Magic and Mechanics
A Reverse Engineering book

First published in 2026
by Scratch Books Ltd.
London

The moral rights of the contributing authors
of this anthology to be identified as such is asserted in
accordance with the Copyright, Designs and Patents Act of 1988.

All rights reserved. No part of this publication
may be reproduced, stored in a retrieval system,
or transmitted in any form or by any means,
electronic, mechanical photocopying, recording,
or otherwise, without the prior permission
of both the copyright owner and the above
publisher of this book.

Cover Design © Alice Haworth-Booth, 2026
Typesetting: Will Dady

Printed and bound on carbon-balanced paper in the UK by CMP Books

ISBN Paperback 978-1-0683555-4-7

Contents

Victory Lap by George Saunders	5
Also There's a Million Dust Specks…:	27
George Saunders on 'Victory Lap'	
The Gloves Are Off by Claire-Louise Bennett	45
Part Of Something Immemorial:	57
Claire-Louise Bennett on 'The Gloves Are Off'	
The Bunker by Mark Haddon	75
Running a Punch and Judy Show:	93
Mark Haddon on 'The Bunker'	
Agata's Machine by Camilla Grudova	109
Keep the Path Submerged:	131
Camilla Grudova on 'Agata's Machine'	
Mr Blythe Esq. by Amber Medland	147
You Don't Want It Too Neat:	167
Amber Medland on 'Mr Blythe Esq.'	
Whoever is There, Come on Through by Colin Barrett	183
Slow Gut Instinct:	209
Colin Barrett on 'Whoever is There, Come on Through'	

Victory Lap

by George Saunders

Three days shy of her fifteenth birthday, Alison Pope paused at the top of the stairs.

Say the staircase was marble. Say she descended and all heads turned. Where was {special one}? Approaching now, bowing slightly, he exclaimed, How can so much grace be contained in one small package? Oops. Had he said *small package*? And just stood there? Broad princelike face totally bland of expression? Poor thing! Sorry, no way, down he went, he was definitely not {special one}.

What about this guy, behind Mr. Small Package, standing near the home entertainment center? With a thick neck of farmer integrity yet tender ample lips, who, placing one hand on the small of her back, whispered, Dreadfully sorry you had to endure that bit about the small package just now. Let us go stand on the moon. Or, uh, in the moon. In the moonlight.

Had he said, *Let us go stand on the moon*? If so, she would have to be like, {eyebrows up}. And if no wry acknowledgment was forthcoming, be like, Uh, I am not exactly dressed for standing on the moon, which, as I understand it, is super-cold?

Come on, guys, she couldn't keep treading gracefully on this marble stairwell in her mind forever! That dear old white-hair in the tiara was getting all like, *Why are those supposed princes making that darling girl march in place ad nausea?* Plus she had a recital tonight and had to go fetch her tights from the dryer.

Egads! One found oneself still standing at the top of the stairs.

Do the thing where, facing upstairs, hand on railing, you hop down the stairs one at a time, which was getting a lot harder lately, due to, someone's feet were getting longer every day, seemed like.

Pas de chat, pas de chat.

Changement, changement.

Hop over thin metal thingie separating hallway tile from living-room rug.

Curtsy to self in entryway mirror.

Come on, Mom, get here. We do not wish to be castrigated by Ms. Callow again in the wings.

Although actually she loved Ms. C. So strict! Also loved the other girls in class. And the girls from school. *Loved* them. Everyone was so nice. Plus the boys at her school. Plus the teachers at her school. All of them were doing their best. Actually, she loved her whole town. That adorable grocer, spraying his lettuce! Pastor Carol, with her large comfortable butt! The chubby postman, gesticulating with his padded envelopes! It had once been a mill town. Wasn't that crazy? What did that even mean?

Also she loved her house. Across the creek was the Russian church. So ethnic! That onion dome had loomed in her window since her Pooh footie days. Also loved Gladsong Drive. Every house on Gladsong was a Corona del Mar. That was amazing! If you had a friend on Gladsong, you already knew where everything was in his or her home.

Jeté, jeté, rond de jambe.

Pas de bourrée.

On a happy whim, do front roll, hop to your feet, kiss the picture of Mom and Dad taken at Penney's back in the Stone Ages, when you were that little cutie right there {kiss} with a hair bow bigger than all outdoors.

Sometimes, feeling happy like this, she imagined a baby deer trembling in the woods.

Where's your mama, little guy?

I don't know, the deer said in the voice of Heather's little sister Becca.

Are you afraid? she asked it. Are you hungry? Do you want me to hold you?

Okay, the baby deer said.

Here came the hunter now, dragging the deer's mother by the antlers. Her guts were completely splayed. Jeez, that was nice! She covered the baby's eyes and was like, Don't you have anything better to do, dank hunter, than kill this baby's mom? You seem like a nice enough guy.

Is my mom killed? the baby said in Becca's voice. No, no, she said. This gentleman was just leaving. The hunter, captivated by her beauty, toffed or doffed his cap, and, going down on one knee, said, If I could will life back into this fawn, I would do so, in hopes you might defer one tender kiss upon our elderly forehead.

Go, she said. Only, for your task of penance, do not eat her. Lay her out in a field of clover, with roses strewn about her. And bestow a choir, to softly sing of her foul end. Lay who out? the baby deer said.

No one, she said. Never mind. Stop asking so many questions.

Pas de chat, pas de chat.

Changement, changement.

She felt hopeful that {special one} would hail from far away. The local boys possessed a certain *je ne sais quoi,* which, tell the truth, she was not *très* crazy about, such as: actually named their own nuts. She had overheard that! And aspired to work for CountyPower because the work shirts were awesome and you got them free.

So ixnay on the local boys. A special ixnay on Matt Drey, owner of the largest mouth in the land. Kissing him last night at the pep rally had been like kissing an underpass. Scary! Kissing Matt was like suddenly this cow in a sweater is bearing down on you, who will not take no for an answer, and his huge cow head is being flooded by chemicals that are drowning out what little powers of reason Matt actually did have.

What she liked was being in charge of her. Her body, her mind. Her thoughts, her career, her future.

That was what she liked.

So be it.

We might have a slight snack.

Un petit repas.

Was she special? Did she consider herself special? Oh, gosh, she didn't know. In the history of the world, many had been more special than her. Helen Keller had been awesome; Mother Teresa was amazing; Mrs. Roosevelt was quite chipper in spite of her husband, who was handicapped, which, in addition, she had been gay, with those big old teeth, long before such time as being gay and First Lady was even conceptual. She, Alison, could not hope to compete in the category of those ladies. Not yet, anyway!

There was so much she didn't know! Like how to change the oil. Or even check the oil. How to open the hood. How to bake brownies. That was embarrassing, actually, being a girl and all. And what was a mortgage? Did it come with the house? When you breast-fed, did you have to like push the milk out?

Egads. Who was this wan figure, visible through the living-room window, trotting up Gladsong Drive? Kyle Boot, palest kid in all the land? Still dressed in his weird cross-country toggles?

Poor thing. He looked like a skeleton with a mullet. Were those cross-country shorts from the like *Charlie's Angels* days or *quoi*? How could he run so well when he seemed to have literally no muscles? Every day he ran home like this, shirtless with his backpack on, then hit the remote from down by the Fungs' and scooted into his garage without breaking stride.

You almost had to admire the poor goof.

They'd grown up together, been little beaners in that mutual sandbox down by the creek. Hadn't they bathed together when wee or some such crud? She hoped that never got out. Because in terms of friends, Kyle was basically down to Feddy Slavko, who walked leaning way backward and was always retrieving things from between his teeth, announcing the name of the retrieved thing in Greek, then re-eating it. Kyle's mom and dad didn't let him do squat. He had to call home if the movie in World Culture might show bare boobs. Each of the items in his lunch box was clearly labeled.

Pas de bourrée.

And curtsy.

Pour quantity of Cheez Doodles into compartmentalized old-school Tupperware dealie.

Thanks, Mom, thanks, Dad. Your kitchen *rocks.*

Shake Tupperware dealie back and forth like panning for gold, then offer to some imaginary poor gathered round.

Please enjoy. Is there anything else I can do for you folks? You have already done enough, Alison, by even deigning to speak to us.

That is so not true! Don't you understand, all people deserve respect? Each of us is a rainbow.

Uh, really? Look at this big open sore on my poor shriveled flank.

Allow me to fetch you some Vaseline.

That would be much appreciated. This thing kills.

But as far as that rainbow idea? She believed that. People were amazing. Mom was awesome, Dad was awesome, her teachers worked so hard and had kids of their own, and some were even getting divorced, such as Mrs. Dees, but still always took time for their students. What she found especially inspiring about Mrs. Dees was that, even though Mr. Dees was cheating on Mrs. Dees with the lady who ran the bowling alley, Mrs. Dees was still teaching the best course ever in Ethics, posing such questions as: Can goodness win? Or do good people always get shafted, evil being more reckless? That last bit seemed to be Mrs. Dees taking a shot at the bowling-alley gal. But seriously! Is life fun or scary? Are people good or bad? On the one hand, that clip of those gauntish pale bodies being steamrolled while fat German ladies looked on chomping gum. On the other hand, sometimes rural folks, even if their particular farms were on hills, stayed up late filling sandbags.

In their straw poll she had voted for people being good and life being fun, with Mrs. Dees giving her a pitying glance as she stated her views: To do good, you just have to decide to do good. You have to be brave. You have to stand up for what's right. At that last, Mrs. Dees had made this kind of groan. Which was fine. Mrs. Dees had a lot of pain in her life, yet, interestingly? Still obviously found something fun about life and good about people, because otherwise why sometimes stay up so late grading you come in next day all exhausted, blouse on backward, having messed it up in the early-morning dark, you dear discombobulated thing?

Here came a knock on the door. Back door. In-ter-est-ing. Who could it be? Father Dmitri from across the way? UPS? FedEx? With *un petit* check *pour Papa*?

Jeté, jeté, rond de jambe.

Pas de bourrée.

Open door, and—

Here was a man she did not know. Quite huge fellow, in one of those meter-reader vests.

Something told her to step back in, slam the door. But that seemed rude.

Instead she froze, smiled, did {eyebrow raise} to indicate: May I help you?

Kyle Boot dashed through the garage, into the living area, where the big clocklike wooden indicator was set at All Out. Other choices included: Mom & Dad Out; Mom Out; Dad Out; Kyle Out; Mom & Kyle Out; Dad & Kyle Out; and All In.

Why did they even need All In? Wouldn't they know it when they were All In? Would he like to ask Dad that? Who, in his excellent totally silent downstairs woodshop, had designed and built the Family Status Indicator?

Ha.

Ha ha.

On the kitchen island was a Work Notice.

Scout: New geode on deck. Place in yard per included drawing. No goofing. Rake areas first, put down plastic as I have shown you. Then lay in white rock. THIS GEODE EXPENSIVE. Pls take seriously. No reason this should not be done by time I get home. This = five (5) Work Points.

Gar, Dad, do you honestly feel it fair that I should have to slave in the yard until dark after a rigorous cross-country practice that included sixteen 440s, eight 880s, a mile-for time, a kajillion Drake sprints, and a five-mile Indian relay?

Shoes off, mister.

Yoinks, too late. He was already at the TV. And had left an incriminating trail of microclods. Way verboten. Could the microclods be hand-plucked? Although, problem: if he went back to hand-pluck the microclods, he'd leave an incriminating new trail of microclods.

He took off his shoes and stood mentally rehearsing a little show he liked to call WHAT IF . . . RIGHT NOW? WHAT IF they came home RIGHT NOW?

It's a funny story, Dad! I came in thoughtlessly! Then realized what I'd done! I guess, when I think about it, what I'm happy about? Is how quickly I self-corrected! The reason I came in so thoughtlessly was, I wanted to get right to work, Dad, per your note!

He raced in his socks to the garage, threw his shoes into the garage, ran for the vacuum, vacuumed up the microclods, then realized, holy golly, he had thrown his shoes into the garage rather than placing them on the Shoe Sheet as required, toes facing away from the door for ease of donnage later.

He stepped into the garage, placed his shoes on the Shoe Sheet, stepped back inside.

Scout, Dad said in his head, has anyone ever told you that even the most neatly maintained garage is going to have some oil on its floor, which is now on your socks, being tracked all over the tan Berber?

Oh gar, his ass was grass.

But no—*celebrate good times, come on*—no oil stain on rug.

He tore off his socks. It was absolutely verboten for him to be in the main living area barefoot. Mom and Dad coming home to find him Tarzaning around like some sort of white trasher would not be the least fucking bit—

Swearing in your head? Dad said in his head. Step up, Scout, be a man. If you want to swear, swear aloud. I don't want to swear aloud.

Then don't swear in your head.

Mom and Dad would be heartsick if they could hear the swearing he sometimes did in his head, such as crap-cunt shit-turd dick-in-the-ear butt-creamery. Why couldn't he stop doing that? They thought so highly of him, sending weekly braggy emails to both sets of grandparents, such as: Kyle's been super-busy keeping up his grades while running varsity cross-country though still a sophomore, while setting aside a little time each day to manufacture such humdingers as cunt-swoggle rear-fuck—

What was wrong with him? Why couldn't he be grateful for all that Mom and Dad did for him, instead of—

Cornhole the ear-cunt.

Flake-fuck the pale vestige with a proddering dick-knee. You could always clear the mind with a hard pinch on your own minimal love handle.

Ouch.

Hey, today was Tuesday, a Major Treat day. The five (5) new Work Points for placing the geode, plus his existing two (2) Work Points, totaled seven (7) Work Points, which, added to his eight (8) accrued Usual Chore Points, made fifteen (15) Total Treat Points, which could garner him a Major Treat (for example, two handfuls of yogurt-covered raisins) plus twenty free-choice TV minutes, although the particular show would have to be negotiated with Dad at time of cash-in.

One thing you will not be watching, Scout, is *America's Most Outspoken Dirt Bikers*.

Whatever.

Whatever, Dad.

Really, Scout? "Whatever"? Will it be "whatever" when I take away all your Treat Points and force you to quit cross-country, as I have several times threatened to do if a little more cheerful obedience wasn't forthcoming?

No, no, no. I don't want to quit, Dad. Please. I'm good at it. You'll see, first meet. Even Matt Drey said—

Who is Matt Drey? Some ape on the football team?

Yes.

Is his word law?

No.

What did he say?

Little shit can run.

Nice talk, Scout. Ape talk. Anyway, you may not make it to the first meet. Your ego seems to be overflowing its banks. And why? Because you can jog? Anyone can jog. Beasts of the field can jog.

I'm not quitting! Anal-cock shit-bird rectum-fritz! Please, I'm begging you, it's the only thing I'm decent at! Mom, if he makes me quit I swear to God I'll—

Drama doesn't suit you, Beloved Only.

If you want the privilege of competing in a team sport, Scout, show us that you can live within our perfectly reasonable system of directives designed to benefit you.

Hello.

A van had just pulled up in the St. Mikhail's parking lot. Kyle walked in a controlled, gentlemanly manner to the kitchen counter. On the counter was Kyle's Traffic Log, which served the dual purpose of (1) buttressing Dad's argument that Father Dmitri should build a soundproof retaining wall and (2) constituting a data set for a possible Science Fair project for him, Kyle, entitled, by Dad, "Correlation of Church Parking Lot Volume vs. Day of Week, with Ancillary Investigation of Sunday Volume Throughout Year."

Smiling agreeably as if he enjoyed filling out the Log, Kyle very legibly filled out the Log:

Vehicle: VAN.
Color: GRAY.
Make: CHEVY.
Year: UNKNOWN.

A guy got out of the van. One of the usual Rooskies. "Rooskie" was an allowed slang. Also "dang it." Also "holy golly." Also "crapper." The Rooskie was wearing a jean jacket over a hoodie, which, in Kyle's experience, was not unusual church-wear for the Rooskies, who sometimes came directly over from Jiffy Lube still wearing coveralls.

Under "Vehicle Driver" he wrote, PROBABLE PARISHIONER.

That sucked. Stank, rather. The guy being a stranger, he, Kyle, now had to stay inside until the stranger left the neighborhood. Which totally futzed up his geode placing. He'd be out there until midnight. What a detriment!

The guy put on a DayGlo-vest. Ah, dude was a meter reader.

The meter reader looked left, then right, leaped across the creek, entered the Pope backyard, passed between the soccer-ball rebounder and the in-ground pool, then knocked on the Pope door.

Good leap there, Boris.

The door swung open.

Alison.

Kyle's heart was singing. He'd always thought that was just a phrase. Alison was like a national treasure. In the dictionary under "beauty" there should be a picture of her in that jean skort. Although lately she didn't seem to like him all that much.

Now she stepped across her deck so the meter reader could show her something. Something electrical wrong on the roof? The guy seemed eager to show her. Actually, he had her by the wrist. And was like tugging.

That was weird. Wasn't it? Something had never been weird around here before. So probably it was fine. Probably the guy was just a really new meter reader?

Somehow Kyle felt like stepping out onto the deck. He stepped out. The guy froze. Alison's eyes were scared-horse eyes. The guy cleared his throat, turned slightly to let Kyle see something.

A knife.

The meter reader had a knife.

Here's what you're doing, the guy said. Standing right there until we leave. Move a muscle, I knife her in the heart. Swear to God. Got it?

Kyle's mouth was so spitless all he could do was make his mouth do the shape it normally did when saying Yes.

Now they were crossing the yard. Alison threw herself to the ground. The guy hauled her up. She threw herself down. He hauled her up. It was odd seeing Alison tossed like a rag doll in the sanctuary of the perfect yard her dad had made for her. She threw herself down.

The guy hissed something and she rose, suddenly docile.

In his chest Kyle felt the many directives, Major and Minor, he was right now violating. He was on the deck shoeless, on the deck shirtless, was outside when a stranger was near, had engaged with that stranger.

Last week Sean Ball had brought a wig to school to more effectively mimic the way Bev Mirren chewed her hair when nervous. Kyle had briefly considered intervening. At Evening Meeting, Mom had said that she considered Kyle's decision not to intervene judicious. Dad had said, That was none of your business. You could have been badly hurt. Mom had said, Think of all the resources we've invested in you, Beloved Only. Dad had said, I know we sometimes strike you as strict but you are literally all we have.

They were at the soccer-ball rebounder now, Alison's arm up behind her back. She was making a low repetitive sound of denial, like she was trying to invent a noise that would adequately communicate her feelings about what she'd just this instant realized was going to happen to her.

He was just a kid. There was nothing he could do. In his chest he felt the lush release of pressure that always resulted when he submitted to a directive. There at his feet was the geode. He should just look at that until they left. It was a great one. Maybe the greatest one ever. The crystals at the cutaway glistened in the sun. It would look nice in the yard. Once he placed it. He'd place it once they were gone. Dad would be impressed that even after what had occurred he'd remembered to place the geode.

That's the ticket, Scout.

We are well pleased, Beloved Only.

Super job, Scout.

Holy crap. It was happening. She was marching along all meek like the trooper he'd known she'd be. He'd had her in mind since the baptism of what's-his-name. Sergei's kid.

At the Russian church. She'd been standing in her yard, her dad or some such taking her picture.

He'd been like, Hello, Betty.

Kenny had been like, Little young, bro.

He'd been like, For you, grandpa.

When you studied history, the history of cultures, you saw your own individual time as hidebound. There were various theories of acquiescence. In Bible days a king might ride through a field and go: That one. And she would be brought unto him. And they would duly be betrothed and if she gave birth unto a son, super, bring out the streamers, she was a keeper. Was she, that first night, digging it? Probably not. Was she shaking like a leaf? Didn't matter. What mattered was offspring and the furtherance of the lineage. Plus the exaltation of the king, which resulted in righteous kingly power.

Here was the creek.

He marched her through.

The following bullet points remained in the decision matrix: take to side van door, shove in, follow in, tape wrists/mouth, hook to chain, make speech. He had the speech down cold. Had practiced it both in his head and on the recorder: *Calm your heart, darling, I know you're scared because you don't know me yet and didn't expect this today but give me a chance and you will see we will fly high. See I am putting the knife right over here and I don't expect I'll have to use it, right?*

If she wouldn't get in the van, punch hard in gut. Then pick up, carry to side van door, throw in, tape wrists/mouth, hook to chain, make speech, etc., etc.

Stop, pause, he said.

Gal stopped.

Fucksake. Side door of the van was locked. How undisciplined was that. Ensuring that the door was unlocked was clearly indicated on the pre-mission matrix. Melvin appeared in his mind. On Melvin's face was the look of hot disappointment that had always preceded an ass whooping, which had always preceded the other thing. Put up your hands, Melvin said, defend yourself.

True, true. Little error there. Should have double-checked the pre-mission matrix.

No biggie.

Joy not fear.

Melvin was dead fifteen years. Mom dead twelve. Little bitch was turned around now, looking back at the house. That willfulness wouldn't stand. That was going to get nipped in the bud. He'd have to remember to hurt her early, establish a baseline.

Turn the fuck around, he said.

She turned around.

He unlocked the door, swung it open. Moment of truth. If she got in, let him use the tape, they were home free. He'd picked out a place in Sackett, big-ass cornfield, dirt road leading in. If fuckwise it went good they'd pick up the freeway from there. Basically steal the van. It was Kenny's van. He'd borrowed it for the day. Screw Kenny. Kenny had once called him stupid. Too bad, Kenny, that remark just cost you one van. If fuckwise it went bad, she didn't properly arouse him, he'd abort the activity, truncate the subject, heave the thing out, clean van as necessary, go buy corn, return van to Kenny, say, Hey, bro, here's a shitload of corn, thanks for the van, I never could've bought a suitable quantity of corn in my car. Then lay low, watch the papers like he'd done with the nonarousing redhead out in—

Gal gave him an imploring look, like, Please don't.

Was this a good time? To give her one in the gut, knock the wind out of her sails?

It was.

He did.

—

The geode was beautiful. What a beautiful geode. What made it beautiful? What were the principal characteristics of a beautiful geode? Come on, think. Come on, concentrate.

She'll recover in time, Beloved Only.

None of our affair, Scout.

We're amazed by your good judgment, Beloved Only. Dimly he noted that Alison had been punched. Eyes on the geode, he heard the little *oof*.

His heart dropped at the thought of what he was letting happen. They'd used goldfish snacks as coins. They'd made bridges out of rocks. Down by the creek. Back in the day. Oh God. He should've never stepped outside. Once they were gone he'd just go back inside, pretend he'd never stepped out, make the model-railroad town, still be making it when Mom and Dad got home. When eventually someone told him about it? He'd make a certain face. Already on his face he could feel the face he would make, like, What? Alison? Raped? Killed? Oh God. Raped and killed while I innocently made my railroad town, sitting cross-legged and unaware on the floor like a tiny little—

No. No, no, no. They'd be gone soon. Then he could go inside. Call 911. Although then everyone would know he'd done nothing. All his future life would be bad. Forever he'd be the guy who'd done nothing. Besides, calling wouldn't do any good. They'd be long gone. The parkway was just across Featherstone, with like a million arteries and cloverleafs or whatever spouting out of it. So that was that. In he'd go. As soon as they left. Leave, leave, leave, he thought, so I can go inside, forget this ever—

Then he was running. Across the lawn. Oh God! What was he doing, what was he doing? Jesus, shit, the directives he was violating! Running in the yard (bad for the sod); transporting a geode without its protective wrapping; hopping the fence, which stressed the fence, which had cost a pretty penny; leaving the yard; leaving the yard barefoot; entering the Secondary Area without permission; entering the creek barefoot (broken glass, dangerous microorganisms), and, not only that, oh God, suddenly he saw what this giddy part of himself intended, which was to violate a directive so Major and absolute that it wasn't even a directive, since you didn't need a directive to know how totally verboten it was to—

He burst out of the creek, the guy still not turning, and let the geode fly into his head, which seemed to emit a weird edge-seep of blood even before the skull visibly indented and the guy sat right on his ass.

Yes! Score! It was fun! Fun dominating a grown-up! Fun using the most dazzling gazelle-like leg speed ever seen in the history of mankind to dash soundlessly across space and master this huge galoot, who otherwise, right now, would be—

What if he hadn't?

God, what if he hadn't?

He imagined the guy bending Alison in two like a pale garment bag while pulling her hair and thrusting bluntly, as he, Kyle, sat cowed and obedient, tiny railroad viaduct grasped in his pathetic babyish—

Jesus! He skipped over and hurled the geode through the windshield of the van, which imploded, producing an inward rain of glass shards that made the sound of thousands of tiny bamboo wind chimes.

He scrambled up the hood of the van, retrieved the geode. Really? Really? You were going to ruin her life, ruin my life, you cunt-probe dick-munch ass-gashing Animal? Who's bossing who now? Gash-ass, jizz-lips, turd-munch—

He'd never felt so strong/angry/wild. Who's the man? Who's your daddy? What else must he do? To ensure that Animal did no further harm? You still moving, freak? Got a plan, stroke-dick? Want a skull gash on top of your existing skull gash, big man? You think I won't? You think I—

Easy, Scout, you're out of control.

Slow your motor down, Beloved Only.

Quiet. I'm the boss of me.

FUCK!

What the hell? What was he doing on the ground? Had he tripped? Did someone wonk him? Did a branch fall? God damn. He touched his head. His hand came away bloody.

The beanpole kid was bending. To pick something up. A rock. Why was that kid off the porch? Where was the knife?

Where was the gal?

Crab-crawling toward the creek.

Flying across her yard.

Going into her house.

Fuck it, everything was fucked. Better hit the road. With what, his good looks? He had like eight bucks total.

Ah Christ! The kid had smashed the windshield! With the rock! Kenny was not going to like that one bit. He tried to stand but couldn't. The blood was just pouring out. He was not going to jail again. No way. He'd slit his wrists. Where was the knife? He'd stab himself in the chest. That had nobility. Then the people would know his name. Which of them had the balls to samurai themselves with a knife in the chest?

None.

Nobody.

Go ahead, pussy. Do it.

No. The king does not take his own life. The superior man silently accepts the mindless rebuke of the rabble. Waits to rise and fight anew. Plus he had no idea where the knife was. Well, he didn't need it. He'd crawl into the woods, kill something with his bare hands. Or make a trap from some grass. Ugh. Was he going to barf? There, he had. Right on his lap.

Figures you'd blow the simplest thing, Melvin said.

Melvin, God, can't you see my head is bleeding so bad? A kid did it to you. You're a joke. You got fucked by a kid.

Oh, sirens, perfect.

Well, it was a sad day for the cops. He'd fight them hand to hand. He'd sit until the last moment, watching them draw near, doing a silent death mantra that would centralize all his life power in his fists.

He sat thinking about his fists. They were huge granite boulders. They were a pit bull each. He tried to get up. Somehow his legs weren't working. He hoped the cops would get here soon. His head really hurt. When he touched up there, things moved. It was like he was wearing a gore cap. He was going to need a bunch of stitches. He hoped it wouldn't hurt too much. Probably it would, though.

Where was that beanpole kid?

Oh, here he was.

Looming over him, blocking out the sun, rock held high, yelling something, but he couldn't tell what, because of the ringing in his ears.

Then he saw that the kid was going to bring the rock down. He closed his eyes and waited and was not at peace at all but instead felt the beginnings of a terrible dread welling up inside him, and if that dread kept growing at the current rate, he realized in a flash of insight, there was a name for the place he would be then, and it was Hell.

Alison stood at the kitchen window. She'd peed herself. Which was fine. People did that. When super-scared. She'd noticed it while making the call. Her hands had been shaking so bad. They still were. One leg was doing that Thumper thing. God, the stuff he'd said to her. He'd punched her. He'd pinched her. There was a big blue mark on her arm. How could Kyle still be out there? But there he was, in those comical shorts, so confident he was goofing around, hands clenched over his head like a boxer from some cute alt universe where a kid that skinny could actually win a fight against a guy with a knife.

Wait.

His hands weren't clenched. He was holding the rock, shouting something down at the guy, who was on his knees, like the blindfolded prisoner in that video they'd seen in History, about to get sword-killed by a formal dude in a helmet.

Kyle, don't, she whispered.

For months afterward she had nightmares in which Kyle brought the rock down. She was on the deck trying to scream his name but nothing was coming out. Down came the rock. Then the guy had no head. The blow just literally dissolved his head. Then his body tumped over and Kyle turned to her with this heartbroken look of, My life is over. I killed a guy.

Why was it, she sometimes wondered, that in dreams we can't do the simplest things? Like a crying puppy is standing on some broken glass and you want to pick it up and brush the shards off its pads but you can't because you're balancing a ball on your head. Or you're driving and there's this old guy on crutches, and you go, to Mr. Feder, your Driver's Ed teacher, Should I swerve? And he's like, Uh, probably. But then you hear this big clunk and Feder makes a negative mark in his book.

Sometimes she'd wake up crying from the dream about Kyle. The last time, Mom and Dad were already there, going, That's not how it was. Remember, Allie? How did it happen? Say it. Say it out loud. Allie, can you tell Mommy and Daddy how it really happened?

I ran outside, she said. I shouted.

That's right, Dad said. You shouted. Shouted like a champ.

And what did Kyle do? Mom said.

Put down the rock, she said.

A bad thing happened to you kids, Dad said. But it could have been worse.

So much worse, Mom said.

But because of you kids, Dad said, it wasn't.

You did so good, Mom said.

Did beautiful, Dad said.

Also There's a Million Dust Specks…:

George Saunders on 'Victory Lap'

George Saunders is an American writer of short stories, essays, novellas, children's books, and novels. His novel *Lincoln in the Bardo* won the Booker Prize in 2017 and his writing has appeared in *The New Yorker*, *Harper's*, *McSweeney's*, and *GQ*.

I wanted to ask George about the amazing use of voice in this story, and the direction he chose for the story's plot.

You have said that this story was partly inspired by Chekhov's 'After the Theatre', and it's fantastic to re-read that knowing it was an influence on you – they have a similar lightness and carnival sense of voice. What was it in Chekhov's story that you felt got you going?

I don't remember what the stories were, but I'd had, in my writing before then, a run of murders and violence – and I just felt I was leaning a little bit on death to make my stories consequential. And then I read that little beautiful Chekhov story and thought, 'Oh, my god, a real writer doesn't have to resort to tragedy. You can just have real emotions – a 16-year-old girl who's feeling exuberant – that should be enough.'

So I tried to do that in my own way, and then of course (because you can't really get away from who you are) when I had written an equivalent amount of text to the Chekhov story I saw that it wasn't anything. It was sort of funny, but somehow it hadn't accomplished what Chekhov's had done: there wasn't that feeling of rising action or import.

So, then I just said, 'Okay, well then maybe something dramatic has to happen, even if it's something violent.' And so it was noticing, and then acceding to, a certain tendency in me that had been exerting itself all along, which is why there was so much death in the earlier stories. So, out of this necessity (the necessity of not being boring) I thought, 'Well, I can't, apparently, do what Chekhov did but I do have two or three pages of pretty compelling teenage-speak: now what happens?'

When you were writing the story, did you have a sense of what you wanted the story to be? Were you pursuing something as you went?

As a general rule, if I do have a feeling like that, I try to push it away, because my feeling is it will make for generally fairly facile ideas. In other words, the idea you might have about a story's future on page one is limited by the current state of your mind whereas, if you revise your ideas about it for eight months, you're going to find so much more depth than you could ever have imagined at the outset. So, if I do have a plan for the story, I try to treat that plan like an annoying friend, like: 'Okay, I see you there, but there are other people here. Let's let them speak.'

So, in 'Victory Lap', I really enjoyed doing her voice in that first section – sometimes you find a voice just within you that you can do pretty naturally and keeps presenting nice jokes and so on.

And then, for me, it's a case of asking how I might make that speech – which has a lot of jokes in it and was, at that moment, just a pretty good monologue – consequential? 'How do I make it so that the speech is either caused by something or is about to cause something?' And that process is very odd because there's nothing particularly intellectual about it; it's more Vaudevillian. You're not trying to suss out a theme at that point at all; it's more along the lines of... well, you've created, say, a guy who says his toe hurts, and then you're going to make him kick something. It's really on that level. I always, internally, invoke the word 'entertainment'. I want it to compel you to keep reading.

I don't remember the exact impulse, in this case, but generally the process for me is: you have the jokes, or the little motions that you like – which you then stand behind and try to just tighten up; make the jokes better, cut out the dull stuff, the place-holding stuff. It's very intuitive and iterative: just editing, editing, editing. And then at some point in that process, a joke will sharpen itself, and then it's as if your text is saying: 'The story's right here, idiot.'

In this case, when Alison made that little speech about people ('If you want to be good, you just have to be good') that was actually me, channelling myself at age seventeen. I recognised my young arrogant self in that idea. Living in suburban Chicago, wondering: 'Why are people drunks? Why are people divorced? They're so stupid! They're so stupid! If only they tried to be good! Uh, that'll never happen to me.'

And so the story became just a way of challenging that facile idea. In a sense you're trying to look for a ripple in an otherwise calm surface. You're re-reading what you've written, to see if that text is posing a dilemma. That ripple in the story's surface can sometimes be a kind of challenge that the story is setting up for you; in this case Alison claims in her naivete that all a person has to do to be good is just will it. And the reader might be feeling: 'Really? Really, kid? You think so?'

Her idea (which was really my 17-year-old idea) made Adult Me think: 'Well, Alison – I don't know about that.' And that's the plot, essentially. Plot can be kind of a call-and-response thing. Take the earlier-mentioned guy with the hurt toe; you, the writer, made a big deal of making his toe hurt... so you do something with that. Recognising that impulse – in the most vaudevillian, stupid way – I had somebody knock on Alison's door. And that was a big moment when that guy knocked on the door. 'Okay so she's in trouble, fantastic!' That guy was, essentially, showing up to challenge her facile ideas about the world.

You've said that these things occur later when you're editing. It makes me think of an expression you use in *A Swim in the Pond in the Rain*, that a good story is one that responds alertly to itself.

Yes, that's right. In this case, the story had her say that rather earnest thing about how to be good. And then it responded to itself.

Where does Kyle come into this? Was he there in the first draft or was he something you needed later?

He was added later. I have an ethos that a story should be as simple as possible; from one point of view, for example. You don't need multiple narrators... until you do. I always want the story to be on a tether – sort of like, the tether of the classical. What's the simplest way we could tell this. I like that feeling of formal discipline.

But then, if I can't do it with one narrator, I'll allow in a second.

At this point – we're at the end of Alison's section and she's opened the door to the abductor – I didn't really want to narrate the whole scene where the guy drags her out and so on. I felt a resistance to what I anticipated would be quotidian narration: 'He reached in, he grabbed her arm, he pulled her out; she resisted.' Ugh. I've learned that if I feel that I don't want to write something, I should try to find a way around it. That's structure: basically, don't write the shit you don't want to write – just go around it.

So, that was why I thought to cut to a new character's POV. Although, my guess is I probably *tried* to get that guy to pull her out the door. But there would have been another issue. I've noticed that, in moments of sudden crisis (like, for example, when you slip and fall on some ice) that inner, narrating voice goes quiet; you're all impulse: you just hit the ice. So, when I tried to write Alison being dragged out, from her point of view, it all seemed nonsensical and false, like: 'Oh no, I'm being pulled out of the door.' It didn't have the kind of fun that that first part had. And what I've found is, if you can't make it come alive... try something else.

I had a neighbourhood in Syracuse in mind where this all 'happened'. It's a lot like the neighbourhood I grew up in, a suburban subdivision. There might be two or three different kinds of floorplans that repeat throughout the whole subdivision. But they mostly all look the same. And something about that made me think: 'Okay, I've said it's a quiet afternoon in that neighbourhood... oh, there's an identical house next door with a sort of identical teenager in it... or at least he's identical in that he is a teenager.'

I remember having some difficulty once I decided to give Kyle his own section, because, after making Alison's voice so distinctive... well, there were drafts where he sounded exactly like she did, you know, just a male Alison, speaking in Valley-speak. And that couldn't be it. So, I played around with different voices for him but I don't have the range to do, you know, two distinct teenage voices – in fact, someone said to me (very charmingly) that the slang Alison uses was never slang in *any* era; it's just kind of a proto-slang.

Anyway, having got myself in this bit of trouble, I blundered towards the idea that you could distinguish two characters by not only voice but also what they are interested in, what they believe in, their ethos. And in his case – again not by design – I came up with this idea of someone who's so intensely overprotected that he has internalised that feeling.

I think I had in mind a family that lived near us in Chicago. Back then, parents did not supervise their kids; they just let them out the door in the morning and hoped they came back at night. But there was one family, of all boys, who were intensely regulated by their father; they literally had this treat system, like Kyle's in the story. We used to make so much fun of them, and they were very embarrassed about it. (Although, as it turned out, three or four of them did end up being Olympians... so there's that.)

It was interesting, this platonic idea of the over-regulated kid; I didn't really think of it as a voice, but of course it does sort of become 'voice-y' the way he talks back and forth with his father, how he's internalized his father's world-view and language and so on.

So, there were two different characters in the sense that one had a very distinctive voice, the other one had a very distinctive set of loyalties, and I now had an external camera on the abduction – Kyle looking out of the window and seeing it. He could describe it fairly pithily because he's just observing it.

I feel like he earned his way into the story for these various technical reasons, that, I think, the reader can feel; the reader can feel when a story has a certain need, and the reader likes it when an aberration in the narrative comes out of a perceived need, rather than just being a bit of whimsicality on the part of the writer.

He's definitely sewn into the fabric of the story. I was interested in the fantastic small details in each character's monologue, how they aggregate and make the character more distinct and the story more 'itself'. How, and at what stage, do you get the pitch of this heightenedness just right? For example, there are details which feel to me almost Dickensian. Do you tighten and adjust these as you edit?

Yes, I'll read through a section and I'm either won over or I'm not. At this stage I'll have a little bit of distance because, even though I wrote it, I'll be reading it fresh. (Or at least trying to.) The 'winning over' for me has so much to do with the language's 'density'. I'm not sure that's quite the right word, but it's like a *fullness* in the language – it's got a compelling sound. You don't have that feeling of being overstuffed with detail, but it's also not flat.

That's a lot of the work of rewriting, just trying to tinker with the sound of the sentences to make sure that they're landing correctly, per my internal monitor. That process often means kicking the jokes up a little. But, sometimes, as you're intimating, it goes too far and you feel the sweat of the midnight oil on it then you have to dial it down a bit. It's all very much to taste.

That process often is where 'character' comes from because – as you change the rhythm by taking things out and putting things in – well, if you put the right things in suddenly… it's character. If the person has a certain thought that's a little bit odd but it sounds nice, well, then, it's not odd, it's just *him*, you know?

It comes from endless tinkering, like the whole thing is kind of vibrating, and you're trying to make it vibrate more beautifully. Which is (in my view) exactly equal to increased specificity, which is exactly equal to 'finding one's voice', which is exactly equal to characters; it's all the same.

At heart, for me, it's all about trying to keep the reader involved and caring.

I know that some proponents of a short story distil everything down to its barest essence. I had the sense in this story, and maybe in other stories of yours, that you're allowing yourself to enjoy the fruit of things that are maybe strictly 'already established'. I wondered if a more anxious writer might have cut and unwittingly reduced the richness of the story?

Basically, my thought is: if it's truly just repetition, you don't want it.

No, of course , it's not really repetition, it's escalation—

Yeah, repetition with a slight twist on it – it's escalatory. Which is what I'm watching for. I don't want repeated beats or repeated descriptions. But you can certainly build on something that seems repetitive to make it escalatory; this can serve characterization.

Say I show someone behaving obsessively about Thing A. If, later, I can expand this notion of 'obsessiveness', and, in that way, find out a little more about the character (as he obsesses over Thing B), well, that is repetition, in a sense, but it's also going to be felt as expansion.

But again... all of this stuff gets sorted by this process of interactive revision. If you get a sense that you've already said something, this encourages you to either cut the line or ramp it up a bit – cause it to go off into some new territory.

I do have a very engineering-based idea about efficiency. But you have to define efficiency with some generosity because efficiency is, let's say, 'Whatever produces some cool effect.' So, if you think of David Foster Wallace... to overwrite in the way he did could be seen, ultimately, as a form of efficiency, because it put that presence in the room. That way of writing fulfilled his intention. There's something about the intentional, hyperbolic overwriting (that kind of playful capaciousness) that I really enjoyed and that was at the heart of who he was as a stylist (and, maybe, as a person).

And in both cases (Alison and Kyle), I *found* those characters in those moments of what, at the time, might have been felt as 'extraneous' writing. For example, when she starts going on about her divorced teacher, I remember thinking, 'Well, maybe that's one too many asides, I'll likely cut this bit later,' but then, in that bit, she says that thing about, 'If you want to be good, just be good.' Which became the linchpin for the whole story. So... I feel that I have to let my characters talk, and overtalk, so I can come to know them better. There's sometimes a sense that too much is too much... unless it's the perfect amount.

Yes, and actually these sections that I queried as being possibly already-established were the bits that made me smile just remembering them, they were the sections that really delight the reader.

And you could also see that as a way of us making an intimate connection between reader and writer. In Turgenev, there's a part where he describes this man as being 'very fond of the ladies'. Or something like that. Then, a little later, he offers a little more (and more specific) description of this guy: whenever he sees a pretty girl, he would start to limp. So, we already have the broad category 'ladies man' in our head, and then we get this very funny, communicative refinement of it. I've known a few 'ladies men' (players, flirts, etc). And then Turgenev surprises me by making me aware of a very specific sub-category within this category – and he's got me. I feel he has a high opinion of me, we might say – he knew I'd get this joke. So, this particularity is one of the reasons I lean in… when I feel the writer has his eye on me in that way.

I think in the UK we don't know a writing tradition that you have in the US. Raymond Carver and Denis Johnson are widely known but we don't talk about writers like Robert Coover and Donald Barthelme as much. There's a good description of their writing [in the introduction to 1979 Granta Anthology of American Writing], that said: 'Stories are no longer strictly a representation of life but rather a verbal fiction. Language assumes a new importance for the American writer… a fascination with the way words structure perception, cognition, experience.'

Are the events and the plot – especially the ending – shaped by the heightenedness of their language? E.g. do

the very heightened idioms of the characters *summon* a much louder and stronger confrontation than in a quieter story like those of Carver or Chekhov?

Someone who I would also put in that tradition is Dickens, for example. Someone like Mrs Jellyby in *Bleak House* is a really liberal woman who is always going on about the plight of the impoverished Africans, but meanwhile her household is a disaster, the kids are falling down the stairs and so on. So funny and so human. But if you went into the house of the real-life corollary for Mrs Jellyby, I bet it would not be as hyperbolic as that. That comes from the Dickensian language.

For as long as I can remember, I've always had strong feelings and perceptions. All very enjoyable. I think I feel things pretty deeply, in other words. And I've always felt that my particular experience of the world was a little bit under-served by minimalism. As somebody who tried very hard to be the next Hemingway, I would write these stories and descriptions in his style although it wasn't how things really felt to me... not the way, say, a party in our neighbourhood felt – it'd been much more crazy and exuberant than that. More uncontrolled and comic and wild.

So when I finally discovered Barthelme – and Barry Hannah was another one – and Dickens, I saw that to really get at the truth of the moment, you might have to move away from the normative, away from the respectability of the quotidian.

It's true that I'm 'sitting at a desk at my laptop'. But also there's a million dust specks on the screen and an upside-down greeting card over here and a bunch of pencils, sharpened at various levels. It's all slightly disordered, and goes beyond (in the moment of observation the (too-simple) construct 'sitting at a desk, at my laptop.') So the question is, what's real? What's realism? All of these things are true functionally, but I just can't get any heat going if I describe it 'as it is' (that is, in a 'normative' prose style). But if I want to describe something... I don't know how it *really* is until I start typing. And when you get Alison's voice, I think that's real. If you could get inside your head or my head, the actual thing going on in there is pretty wild. But, to be honest... I believe in this approach because I have more fun doing it – and I have more fun doing it because I believe in it; it's all part of the same package.

I think if you talk to Barthelme, he didn't experience reality the way Carver did; he felt that there was more to it, or that there was, let's say, 'difference' to it... and language is the doorway to that.

I wanted to ask a question about the plot. I wondered whether this story is something of a Hollywood plot – an unpopular teenager redeems himself through a moment of bravery. It's something I imagine I'd see in an American film and I wanted to ask why steer close to such an often-told story?

It's more the other way around. I was telling this weird story, and then I perceived within it a hint of the familiar, and was gratified because if I have this weird comic language that I'm asking you to accept, you need some kind of grounding, or recognizable structure. So, it was exciting to be writing this strange monologue-based story and suddenly find this more traditional rescue story emerging from within it. And then, when I was done, I felt: 'Well, such things as tragedy and heroism do happen, you know? So, I'm glad some of that showed up in my story.'

It's an occasion for heroism, and I think at that point in my life I felt that a lot of fiction I was reading didn't really believe that heroism was possible. As a parent, I see all kinds of heroism, and I think when you start pretending that things that you are witnessing and living by (not only heroism but kindness and fellow-feeling and so on, the possibility for transcendence) don't exist, you get into kind of a strange literary landscape.

So, I was happy that it started to look like something familiar, actually, to be honest. And I think of it, not so much Hollywood, but, maybe, 'archetypal'. There's a damsel in distress, essentially or, actually, a person in trouble, and I'd have never started saying, 'I'm going to write a story about a damsel in distress' but having discovered that I'd done so, I was kind of happy – like, people will at least feel there's some import here. Because I've written and read a lot of stories that are just really clever internal monologues where nothing substantial occurs, and I'm not so interested in those.

So, like other stories in *The Tenth of December,* this story is a rescue story. And in that period, those types of stories kept coming to me. I'm not sure why. But, at the time, I felt that certain valences in my actual life were under-represented in life. Like: sometimes people actually do rise to the occasion.

This sensibility that doesn't believe in heroism – is that something like an existentialism or like a 'nothing really matters' relativism?

Yeah, maybe. Often, I think it's just a technical defect – it's harder to write a story that asks, for example, what real heroism might look like. Some middling stories hide behind the idea that 'nothing matters and what if it did?' Writers, including me, understandably flinch from being corny or facile or moralistic. But then, if you went to that writer's house, you know, you'd see that writer trying to be a good person, to make life nice for his family, and so on.

Maybe I'm talking more to myself as a young writer, who was afraid of being corny or mawkish and so became more of a cynic on the page than I actually was in real life.

After we had our kids, it really struck me that, at the end of the day, people function by caring. That's what we do. And fiction or literature could be about what impedes our caring. We wake up in the morning and *want* to be cheerful and loving and helpful, we want things to go well. Okay, but life is such that it doesn't always go as planned. That could be the seed of fiction.

In a sense here, I'm being Alison: saying, 'To be good all you have to do is be good.' Or, you know: 'All people aspire to be loving and kind.' Which is true… but clearly things go awry with that plan, on scales large and also global. So, then your job as a fiction writer is to go, 'Okay, let me challenge that.' If it was easy, everybody would be doing it. Why are, then, some people not loving, not kind? And we find out, of course, that being loving and kind is vastly more nuanced and challenging and complicated. That might be one thing stories are for – to complicate dangerously facile bromides.

Yes, one of those nuances is when Kyle very nearly goes too far and it becomes more than him simply saving the day.

Yes. If you say, 'Let's have this character save the day,' the question becomes: 'How?' A big challenge for me in writing this story was that I had to ask: '*How* can this guy possibly save the day?' Well, and also, given who Kyle was, 'How can *this* guy save the day?' And pretty soon it became clear that he had to save the day, somehow. Otherwise, I'm going to put this very sweet girl in incredible danger from this really huge malevolent guy, and then I'm going to have another pretty sweet teenager just watch as she's destroyed? Jeez, that's cruel.

So, somewhere, there's a lot of very (unintentionally) funny early stuff where I was just trying to figure out *how* Kyle could possibly intervene. All very improbable. (He taunts the abductor so harshly that the abductor chases him around the block, allowing Alison to make her escape. That kind of thing.) Then what was so fun and surprising for me in the writing was that, when he did intervene, he had to do it against all that programming that I'd put in there for no reason (originally) other than to be funny.

So, that's the story responding to itself – I put his restrictive parents in there without any rationale; it was just for fun. But then (later, unplanned by me) it became essential to the action and meaning of the story.

Returning to this story after probably over ten years, what do you think of it? Have you read it again recently?

Oh, yes – this used to be my performance piece, I'd often read it aloud. So, yeah, I like it. I still like it. It's an education to go back to my work. When I first finish a story, I'm very fond of it and it seems... perfect. A perfectly crafted masterpiece. But when I read it years later, I think, 'Oh my god, do you know, George, that you're quite an excessive person?' But I like that feeling. I like being original, even a little bit, even if it's an odd, misshapen kind of originality. I feel like, 'Wow, that Saunders guy was really working through something. He's odd. Odd but intense.'

I'm good with that. I like that the story is not afraid, that it's trying to do something new and not necessarily 'realistic'. I'm very happy making these very cartoonish, excessive people. Although at the time, it felt like I was being very meticulous about recording the reality that was playing out in my head. But you know I'm okay with it.

Yes, we really get the sense of your reality in this. Could you say what you learned from writing this story or your writing at that time of *The Tenth of December* stories? I know you used a minimalist almost Hemingway-style in your youth, but was there another movement of you becoming yourself?

Well, I'm not there yet. Sometimes you write a book to get something out of your system. This book was followed by *Lincoln in the Bardo*, so I think these stories allowed me to say, 'If nothing else, I have really been playful.' My approach to character was to be way over the top in the language and the jokes and everything. I felt like I was really inhabiting a particular contemporary, performative mode of sorts, you know? Another way to say it is that I was being a very particular, performative, version of myself.

Then, having done that in that book, I felt that I didn't want to repeat myself, which opened up some doors of permission for me to write the Lincoln book. Although it also had a lot of voices, they were a little more controlled; in order to make those many voices and distinguish them, I had to do actually less with voiciness. So, it was, maybe, like having a big drunken party and the next day thinking that a quiet game of checkers might be nice: it freed me from the effusiveness and let me be a little bit more workman-like for the next book, which was what was required to get that book done.

Could you say, looking at your work, what is it you think you want to do with your writing? What is it your writing is 'after'?

It's a good question... I love it when somebody like you, who I don't know, picks up a story and gets delighted or surprised, even if they don't necessarily *love* it. It's just the natural performer or the ham in me that likes my work to feel excessive and, hopefully, original, in some small way.

Within that, I think there can sometimes be that magical 'reaching over' to you, the reader – with your joys and issues and concerns. It feels like me reaching out across time and space and going, 'Oh God, yes, me too.' That feeling of 'Life is hard, brother, but we're both in it.' To me it's such a powerful thing, more than success or publication. But there's also an element of celebration: 'Life is gorgeous, isn't it? Aren't we lucky to be here?'

When I was a kid, I had these two really funny uncles from Texas; they could do characters, and I remember the feeling of them coming into our house, doing a voice, making everyone laugh. The characters they were doing were very big and comic, but they could also be insightful, in that Shakespearean jester way. Now, it seems to me that, in my writing, I am trying to be like them. I found that I couldn't hit that pitch (of comedy and insight and joyful overflow) in Hemingway mode: by being correct or constrained or measuredly insightful about something small. I found that, for me, it's more about play. If I play, then you hopefully like to watch me play, and then we're playing together.

It's a pretty small thing, really, this interchange between reader and writer, but it's tangible, and I believe that, yeah, that's enough.

They could put that on your gravestone and you'd be happy?

I think so. Although it's kind of a lot of words. Maybe I'd choose, 'Wow, that was fun.'

The fun is: we're looking at the story together, reader and writer.

I can look at 'Victory Lap' fairly objectively now. It's a non-random construction; it's a machine that responds to itself. It's like, I'd say – there's life in it – but it's not a mirror. And when people respond to it, they're partly Alison – they have a part of themselves that is an Alison corollary. But they're also partly Kyle (they have a Kyle corollary). They might even, god forbid, have a bad-guy corollary.

Re-reading the story now, there's some weird satisfaction in seeing that all play out – I feel the writer is involved in the story and is trying to make it lively and truthful and has forgotten, for a little while, about making the story orderly or conventional – I feel I'm a writer who is nicely out of control because he's very invested in the outcome and is trying to veer away from the habitual.

All of that is to say: I feel myself in there, but not necessarily the self I get up and carefully construct every day – there's something wild and authentic and even a little unseemly going on.

It's like model railroad towns; why is it fun to go into someone's basement and look at the elaborate railroad town they built? Because it *is* fun, especially if the town is coherent in some way. So, I think art is just a mysterious thing. Why do we like it? Why do we, sometimes, live for it? But I think, ultimately, it's a form of reassurance that your experience isn't so different from mine.

The Gloves Are Off

by Claire-Louise Bennett

When my friend who lives nearby called over I was outside again on the steps this time taking the disposable barbeque I'd bought earlier in the day up to where there's a stone alcove — I was quite sure he wouldn't spot me straight away and seeing oneself being looked for wrenches the heart oh ever so gently and must be one of my favourite occurrences — I thought I'd get to look at him lean his bicycle on mine, which was in the usual place, and go into my cottage, where of course he wouldn't find me. As it was he saw me immediately — before he'd even dismounted his bike — which rather spoiled things, and since I hadn't expected that at all I was caught somewhat off guard which I swiftly concealed by holding the disposable barbeque out vertically, right out in front of my face, a peculiar reflex which more or less pulled me together. What are you doing with that, he said — putting it somewhere, I said, and that's what I did.

He came on up the steps then and sat down on the stone alcove, near to where I'd put the disposable barbeque — we didn't say anything about it, perhaps because I'd already mentioned it on the phone earlier on, in which case he already knew I'd nothing yet to put on it so there was nothing much to say. He said he was fed up, or something like that, and I said I was too — he seemed to think it had to do with how the weather had been the same for two weeks. I was inclined to believe it had more to do with how our lives had been more or less the same for much longer. I really despise having thoughts like that since I can't ever reliably ascertain where it is exactly such ideas arise from, I didn't feel like going into it anyway and supposed neither of us would benefit from it very much even if I were to. We looked at a massive dragonfly for a while, it was very easy to follow because of how bright and big it was and I was as good as mounted between its perfectly Edwardian wings when my friend asked me to make him some coffee, which was fine by me and down I went. He came inside to drink it and I lolled against the wall by the window rather sulkily — it was too late in the day for me to have coffee you see, so I resorted to making marks on the wall with my irked fingers and flashed him sidelong glances now and then. He asked me if my water was hot and I said I didn't know, probably I said — his shower hadn't been fixed, which didn't surprise me in the least because when it stopped working before he didn't notify the landlord and I'm not sure what would have happened if he hadn't had an accident which meant I took care of things, including going around to his landlord and telling him about the shower and asking him to get a new sofa because the one that was there was old and lopsided and would probably be very bad for someone trying to heal a broken femur. Turn on the immersion, he said, which I did, and then I turned it off again and back on, then off, flipping the switch, on and off, on and off, on and on, and then I stopped and said now you don't know whether it's on or off do you, which cheered him up. It's on, he said, and he was quite right.

While my friend was having a nice shower I took the bowl down to the compost bin and it was comforting to see just my blanket on the washing line in the shade. The compost bin is really filling up and I couldn't get a good look at its contents like I customarily do because it's got very lively in there. There were just way too many flies this time, and I suppose now it'll only get busier and busier and some days I'll hardly want to turn and lift the lid at all. On the way back I put the empty bowl on the bench near the pond and sat down beside it. I think I should probably have just kept it in my hands really and held it in my lap because sitting next to the bowl felt really peculiar and it took some effort on my part not to glance down at it and ask it how it was doing. My neighbour's blanket was on that part of the ground nearest the pond where there is no grass just small stones, gravel I suppose, except I think gravel tends to make a noise and slide around a bit whereas this stuff is completely embedded and doesn't make any sound at all. Evidently my neighbour's blanket has been down on the ground for quite some time and throughout a lot of rainfall because it's practically enmeshing the stones and in fact in places it's difficult to tell the difference between the stones and the coarse and murky weave of the blanket, just lying there, like a flung-off reptilian carapace. The sight of it gave me the shivers actually and it was soon obvious that sitting on the bench was not very helpful and would improve nothing so I picked up the bowl and went on up the path towards my cottage. It was as if there was nothing left for me to see. I looked at all the leaves from last year on the main steps which lead up to the gate where the post box perches and I don't know how many times now I've heard my landlady's sister comment upon them.

It's quite true; I don't do anything really. Any progressive human being with access to this much land would surely set about growing an impressive selection of vegetables right away. If I wasn't so lazy I could be enjoying delicious homegrown produce for months on end. It crosses my mind now and then of course; in spring the supermarkets have a habit of putting shelving units full of grow-your-own gardening kits right in front of the automatic doors, you can't miss them really, but in a strange way these packages deter rather than inspire me. They frequently have a lot of excessively cheerful writing on them and look so manufactured I just can't conceive how anything natural and enduring could possibly spring from them. Sometimes I've gone as far as to shove a beginner's pack into my basket but by the time I've reached the dairy section I've zero hope left that whatever it contains will amount to anything worthwhile so I take it out and dump it among the spotlit speciality cheeses, which is probably very bad of me.

No weeding, no trimming, very little sweeping; when it comes to external upkeep I really am a relentless little lazy bones. Though when the thatchers were here they left behind such a mess, and straw or reeds or whatever they are kept coming into the cottage, which made me so cross I had to get out there eventually and clear it up as best I could. My prolonged indolence in this case was I think quite reasonable since it mostly consisted of disappointment in fact. The thatchers arrived to do the roofs around the same time I'd begun painting over my bathroom walls which were dark green in the beginning, so dark and porous looking that sometimes at night their surfaces seemed to disappear completely and it was as if I might actually be able to glide my hands and arms and the rest of me far into the wall and enter some other place that probably requires small sharp weapons and a hunk of kick-ass cheese. However, after a shower, when there was condensation running all over them, it was quite a different story. It was a real little squelch hole then, and I often suspected newts and frogs and big-bellied spiders were peering at my dripping nakedness from behind the clammy glistening beams. The yellow I chose in order to give the walls a more respectable dimension was very smart indeed, what I consider to be a Renaissance yellow, or, if you prefer, matador yellow. I presented a sample to my landlady and she nestled it into her new handbag so she could take it to her sister who hadn't been feeling too well and they both agreed it was very striking. Imagine what it will look like with the grey slate floor, I said, and she agreed that it would look very stylish indeed with the grey slate floor. I got an enormous tub of it which was as well because I had to apply endless coats in order to cover up that green which just seemed hell-bent on showing through and I didn't want so much as a trace of it remaining because of the beastly way it completely undermined the yellow and made it seem folksy and psychedelic, and of course that was not the effect I was after at all.

As might be expected I was in the bathroom all day every day for perhaps two weeks — I think I may have gone off somewhere for a few days before it was quite finished, so it could be that it was longer than two weeks even — and, naturally, given the odorous nature of my task I had the window open at all times. This meant I could keep a close eye on the thatchers, unbeknownst to them, and I often saw them gawking at one of the girls who was living in the main cottage at the time. I didn't find their smutty high jinks the least bit surprising and thought the way my neighbours made such a fuss over the thatchers really very misplaced and naive. They seemed to be out there every five minutes, taking photographs of the thatchers and with both hands bestowing upon them great big mugs of tea — as if they were dauntless chieftains from days of yore. I don't know why it is that people tend to assume that artisanal tradesmen who work with natural materials according to traditional methods are wholesome souls with salt-of-the-earth sensibilities. These two, as far as I could see, were a right dirty pair and I seemed to be the only one who sensed it which was interesting for the reason that they spoke Irish all day long so I was also the only one who, strictly speaking, didn't have a clue what they were talking about. They came to the door one day with my landlady who wanted to talk to me about the struts, there on either side, which were in very bad shape apparently and needed replacing. After a bit my landlady leaned in and asked me what my Irish was like and the thatchers looked terribly pleased with themselves and began to chuckle. Well, I said, it's funny you should ask — it turns out I can understand quite a bit actually. Is that right, she said, and the two of them soon zipped up their triumphal tittering, needless to say. And what kind of nonsense would this pair be talking, she said. Oh I couldn't repeat it, I said, absolutely shocking — especially this one, I said, and nodded at the shorter one who went very red and slack and I knew he was as guilty as could be. They both shuffled about in the small space and began patting the shoddy struts with their hands while looking right up at the sky, as if it were the legs of a giraffe they stood between. Overall I had no truck with the thatchers — I hope you know what you're doing, I'd call up to them now and then, which delighted the taller one and completely mystified the shorter one. Indeed, it wasn't the crafty demeanour and furtive buffoonery of the thatchers that was a cause of disappointment to me; it was the origin of the materials they used to replenish the thatch that was the real let-down.

The reeds were in great big beautiful round bundles all across the driveway, and in the evening, before going home, the thatchers would cover them over so they'd stay snug and dry throughout the night. I'd inferred the reeds had been sourced from somewhere not too far away, along the River Shannon most likely, and that was something I liked to think about actually. I liked to think about all the little fishes that had nudged around and prodded at the reeds here and there. And I liked to think about the bigger fish, pike for example, that had occasionally swished past deep down and set them off nervously swaying, for miles and miles and miles perhaps. And the adrenalised coots spun out by the whirlpool of their own incessant rubbernecking and the hot-headed moorhens zigzagging to and fro. And the swans' flotilla nests resplendent with marbled eggs. And the sly-bones heron in a world of his own. And the skaters and the midges and the boatmen and the dragonflies and the snails and the spawn, and who knows what else the susurrant reeds are raided with. Are these reeds, I said to the taller one one day. They are, he said. Where they from, I said. Turkey, he said. Turkey, I said. That's right, he said. How come, I said. It's cheaper, he said. Really, I said. Because to tell you the truth I couldn't quite believe my ears and sometime later, weeks after in fact, I still wasn't convinced so I looked into the matter and almost immediately discovered that the Shannon River and the many tributaries that flow into it had indeed been a prime source of water reed until about twenty years ago. Since then widespread use of intensive farming methods has increased the use of fertilizers and these run down from the fields with the copious rain and contaminate the waterways so that while the nitrates force the reeds to grow fast and long they grow too fast and too long and so are actually quite brittle and pretty well useless and in fact wouldn't last very long at all up on a roof. And that's the reason why.

It seemed to me actually that it was high time I cleaned off the old leaves from the main steps so I went into the kitchen and got the broom and took it up to the top step. Now, I do not know if my method for clearing off the leaves was the best approach since it involved sweeping the leaves from the top step down to the next step and then sweeping both lots of leaves onto the following step, and so on. Probably it would have been better to have used a pan to collect the leaves from each step, but it wasn't that important to me to do it the best way and I quite liked how the heap spilled and prospered like a big tumbling ogre as I made my way down the steps with the broom. I was almost at the last step when my friend came out and just stood there. Did you have a nice shower, I said. Yeah, he said. About time, I said, and then I told him to go and get a wheelbarrow, which he didn't look altogether pleased about. Briefly I had thought that perhaps a little concerted effort might shake us out of our ennui but in this respect our natures are quite distinct and I knew he'd demonstrate no enthusiasm or initiative whatsoever so I gave up the idea that this might be an invigorating endeavour and simply continued to tell him what to do instead. I don't like gardening, he said, we're not gardening, I said. What are we doing then, he said. Tidying up, I said. Soon as that was done I nudged the broom over the large rock to loosen leaves caught up in a contorted tangle of grappling stems — what is this anyway, I said — it seemed dead, whatever it was, so I yanked at it until it leapt loose and the rock became completely clear and was something naked and impressive. I could tell my friend could see no point to what I was doing — I bundled what I'd ripped up into the wheelbarrow and told him to empty it then I went off to find tools — he would be going soon and I wanted to know how it would be to go on doing what I was doing without anyone around.

I found secateurs and shears and since I was in the business of sprucing things up I was thrilled with both — particularly the secateurs because although I'd seen the shears here and there — in quite hazardous places it must be said — I hadn't known anything about the secateurs so they were a real bonus. There were a lot of rampant brambles, and other things on the wane. It had never before occurred to me to do anything about them, it didn't seem to be any of my business to tell you the truth — interfering is something I really loathe in almost all its applications. So, I was trimming — pruning you might call it — and pulling up weeds and patting the soil back down, and I soon felt like one of those ladies I'd see from the car window on the way to my grandparents' house with their ample backsides and baggy gardening gloves when I was much smaller. This is mindless, I thought, and very unflattering — stop it at once. But I didn't stop because I was so curious to find out what changed if I carried on. I had an uneasy relationship with my task, that is for sure, and I had to go on telling myself things like everything will grow back, it helps the little plants come forth, all the big stuff is almost dead anyway — you don't ever have to do this again was the final assurance I offered myself — but if you don't do something today, now, how will you find anything out about how you feel? I couldn't continue with the tools so put them down and carried on with my hands, which were ungloved, and very soon they were stinging, which was fair. Come on then, I thought, and watched as my hands tore around indiscriminately. Is this kind of frenzied pulling and wrenching what happens once you begin? Perhaps I really hate all this stuff and it is a very normal and human thing to wish to crush it. But no, not that, I wasn't pitting myself against nature or anything as hammy as that — I was suddenly desperate to get rid of all this dishevelled foliage, it's true, but the reason I soon realised was because I wanted to get to bare soil — I missed it — it was all covered over and I wanted so much to push everything aside and see the earth. I'd had quite enough of leaves and flowers, all that rustling and blooming and liquid light, it was time for all that to pack itself off really. Except of course it doesn't go anywhere it just lies around like a lot of burst things and shrivels and withers and becomes very soggy and swamp-like. Oh, fuck the leaves and fuck the flowers! I want to see naked trees and hear the earth gasp and settle into a warm and tender mass of radiant darkness. I want to see the marks of hooves, not eleventh hour disposable barbeques. I want most of all to get inside there. That's right, that's always been true. It's the first thing I can remember. Standing at the back window, looking at the lawn, and knowing exactly everything beneath it and wanting to get back there. You don't know how passionate it is down there.

I believe that's where I lost my heart.

Out beyond and way back and further past that still. And such was it since. But after all appearances and some afternoons misspent it came to pass not all was done and over with. No, no. None shally shally on that here hill. Ah, but that was idle then and change was not an old hand. No, no. None shilly shilly on that here first rung. So, much girded and with new multitudes, a sun came purple and the hail turned in a year or two. And that was not all. No, no. None ganny ganny on that here moon loose. Turns were taken and time put in, so much heft and grimace, there, with callouses, all along the diagonal. Like no other time and the time taken back, that too like none other that can be compared to a bovine heap raising steam, or the eye-cast of a flailing comet. Back and forth, examining the egg spill and the cord fray and the clowning barnacle. And all day with no break to unwrap or unscrew or squint and flex or soak the brush. No, no. None flim flim on that here cavorting mainstay. From tree to tree and the pond there deepening and some small holes appearing and any number of cornstalks twisting into a thing far from corn. That being the case there was some wretched plotting, turned to stone, holding nothing. No, no. None rubby rubby on that here yardstick. Came then from the region of silt and aster, all along the horse trammel and fire velvet, first these sounds and then their makers. When passed betwixt and entered fully, pails were swung and notches considered. There was no light. No, none. None wzm wzm on that here piss crater. And it being the day, still considered. Oh, all things considered and not one mentioned, since all names had turned in and handed back. Knowing this the hounds disbanded and knowing that the ground muddled headstones and milestones and gallows and the almond-shaped buds of freshest honeysuckle. And among this chafing tumult fates were scrambled and mortality made untidy and pithy vows took themselves a breather. This being the way and irreversible homewards now was a lifted skeletal thing of the past, without due application or undue meaning. No, no. None shap shap on that here domicile shank. From right foot to left, first by the firs, then by the river, hung and loitered, and the blaze there slow to come. All night waking with no benefit of sleeping and the breath cranking and the heart-place levering and the kerosene pervading but failing to jerk a flame from out any one thing. No, none. None whoosh whoosh on that here burnished cunt. Oh, the earth, the earth and the women there, inside the simpering huts, stamped and spiritless, blowing on the coals. Not far away, but beyond the way of return.

Part Of Something Immemorial:

Claire-Louise Bennett on 'The Gloves Are Off'

Claire-Louise Bennett's debut book, *Pond*, was shortlisted for the Dylan Thomas Prize in 2016. Her debut novel, *Checkout 19,* was part of *The New York Times* 10 Best Books of 2022.

In our conversation about 'The Gloves are Off', we spoke about how her ideas influence, and are separate from, her writing.

'The Gloves are Off' deals with the fleeting moments and thoughts that would form only the background incidents in a more plot-led story. I wondered what you wanted *this* story to be like?

I know when I was writing *Pond* I did have quite strong ideas about what it was I wanted to create and where the focus would be, and that was a deliberate move away from the typical cornerstones of a story, the fiction we're familiar with, which is quite character and plot-based.

I was interested in picking up on elements of day-to-day life that maybe don't get so much attention or if they do they tend to get it in a metaphorical way – in the service of illustrating something bigger or more significant rather than just the thing itself.

Yes, like an objective correlative?

Yeah, everything's got a mirror, it has a function in a bigger schema.

So why did you want to focus on these 'incidental' details of the mundane?

I suppose it is a way of questioning the hierarchy of values – what's important and what isn't, and what gives us a sense of who we are, and where we are, and where we should derive that from. In *Speak, Memory*, Nabokov refers to the dimensional scale of the world, and that's an interesting notion to consider. He identified a meeting-place between imagination and knowledge – and you get to that point by reducing the larger things and increasing the smaller ones. For him, there was something intrinsically artistic about that. It's an extraordinary way of going beyond the mundane without moving into magical realism or fantasy or what have you.

I was thinking about all that a great deal – the mundane and the incidental and this idea of paying attention to what is immediately around us: it's very important, and it has been very important at different times throughout literary history. One moment I think about and draw on is the modernist period, when there was very much a lack of faith in external frameworks to give one a sense of direction and meaning, whether that be religious or societal or whatever it might be.

During the modernist period, in the early twentieth century, people didn't really have much faith in those things anymore for quite obvious reasons, and so they were really looking to themselves. I think subjective experience became very important for individuals and particularly individual artists. They were saying, 'What is there around me? What can I see and how does that make me feel and think and can I establish a reality from that?'

So I was thinking about that, possibly prompted by having just come out of academia – which, in its own way, is very much an external world of significance, its webs of significance are quite distinct and separate from one's own inner world. So I needed to re-establish myself in the immediate world a little bit and leave that theoretical realm behind. It made sense to me to work in this mode of just noticing and recording what was going on. I think that was the process. It wasn't that I sat down and started mapping out stories with particular intentions. It was just a mode of being and creating and thinking. Which these stories arose out of.

When you mention reality, are you trying to capture and render something like a realism then? Like a verisimilitude?

No, I don't know if I'm trying to do that. I suppose I've a slight frustration with some of the established ways of thinking about what a story should be, or what fiction should be presenting – and particularly that realist mode.

What we tend to think of as realism is itself very constructed and not especially realistic. And I guess it's a modernist feature as well, that idea that you don't really know what you're doing until you've done it.

Is your writing a process of discovery?

Yes, it means nothing is taken for granted. Nothing is *already* there. My relationship to certain things is a bit nebulous. That's why, in the story, she expresses this frustration with the flowers and the other things; the things that have come to fruition; the things that exist; the things that are on the surface; the things that have been cultivated. And you can see she's fed up with it at this stage. She's like, 'Oh, just fuck off. I want them to go and there to be bare earth.'

There's that wonderful sense of that brown, empty space, although it's not empty. It's always very rich and very potent – there's just nothing there *then*. It's that sense of what's dormant, what's beneath, rather than what's been cultivated and planned and arranged, the flowers and gardens. And they're lovely, but she thinks, 'Well, that's had its time now. I've had enough of it.'

I guess in a way that might be a parallel with my attitude to the short story. There are established ideas about what it looks like and the format of it, because there are very strong ideas about the short story in particular. It's like it already exists, and you think, 'Well, if it already exists, I don't know why I'm writing one.' It just feels weird so you do want to just start from scratch, start with bare earth, and excavate.

And her dumping the gardening starter kit in the cheese aisle, is that again her reacting to the artifice? She doesn't like the readymade-ness of it – is that linked to what you're talking about?

Yeah, she's quite distrustful of it, because it looks so pristine and not at all wild. How could anything really fertile and wonderful and vibrant come out of something like that? It seems a bit incongruous.

Yeah, you do wonder sometimes – these steps to writing a story, they just seem so formulaic. And actually that makes me very anxious – in the same way the gardening kit does, because I know I can't follow directives very well, I always make a mistake, probably because I feel so tense and self-conscious about it. I don't want to be too aware of what I'm doing – be that growing something or writing something, it makes me uneasy and sort of impatient. I sort of have to trick myself into it. I tell myself I'm not really doing anything, I'm just playing about a bit. And weirdly approaching it like that means I stay close to the thing, all the way, and that's very important. I suppose if you don't have guidelines or instructions you remain vigilant, you're having to figure out with every faculty you have the nature of the thing.

We've spoken a bit about where you started from. When you finish a story, how do you come to get to the stage of thinking, 'That's good, that's enough, I'll stop working on that now.' If you're starting off on a process of discovery, do you get to the stage of having discovered something? Or, what is the quality that your writing should have for it to feel finished?

I don't know where that feeling derives from, but at some point I feel the story is autonomous in some way. I think it achieves a certain fullness, a pair of eyes. I feel it exists independently, like it's a separate entity and wants me to leave it alone now. There's a sense that it could carry on, but it carries on without words. Like the words now are done, and it – whatever it is – doesn't need any more of them. I've put enough words on whatever it is. And that's it. Words I attempt to add after that point slide off it. It's not about trying to achieve perfection, or even completion. There comes a point when it looks back at me, with quite disdainful eyes actually, and I have to leave it alone then, I have to let it go.

In a way, you say this story has a very strong plotline as, even though chronologically it dots around, it charts her mounting tension, from trying to keep her emotions in check, until they mount and she becomes suddenly desperate at the end. Was this drama unconscious in you as you wrote this?

Yeah, I think probably it was. I don't think I'd set out to write something like that, because if I did, it would end up being very bad probably. I think what else was interesting to me at this time – and something that I explored throughout *Pond* – was this idea that the things that she's feeling, are they personal? Or are they part of something bigger? Is she a function of a bigger pool of feeling? Her sense that, 'I'm not really going to know how I feel unless I do something.' It's that engagement with the physical world around her that gives her some clue about what's happening in her own inner world, which is connected with this larger pool. They all interpenetrate each other. Which is something that's explored a lot throughout the book, generating some quite dramatic moments, because this sense of the inner and outer become so blurred she's almost in danger. She's not really looking out for herself because she's not entirely contained within herself.

I occasionally wonder if this action, this clearing she's doing, is what's actually bringing on this feeling of desperation, rather than the desperation being the thing that motivates the clearing. It's hard to say – a simple action repeated over and over is a very powerful thing really, it can work you up into a frenzy, because it's as if you are attempting to evoke, or provoke, something. You want this impulse to be met in some way. Many years ago, I copied out a line from Breton's *L'Amour Fou*, it goes, 'Sometimes, for example, wishing for a visit of a particular woman I have found myself opening a door, then shutting it, then opening it again.' That line haunts me. I can see it – the man, the action, the little scene – like one of those very early black and white cartoons that jump a bit. It's very powerful, the idea that this repeated action will eventually cause what he desires most to occur. How can it be left unanswered? It's absurd, and tragic, very beautiful really.

I wanted to ask you about this story in particular because it was rare in *Pond* that the narrator has an interaction with another person. Although then, as I read it again, I realised the friend proves an obstacle to the story; she only really gets into the gardening and thinking about herself once he's gone. I wondered why the friend was there, what he brings to the story?

I don't know what he brings to the story but I think it brings something to the situation which I guess is a separate thing? I like his arrival at the beginning because it sets up the idea that it will be about the two of them in some way but then it really isn't.

But it's also that sometimes we have people in our lives who come and go quite regularly day to day, without it being a big deal. They might just come round and have a shower and a cup of tea and then go off again – they might not be the main event really.

I was moving away from this idea that she was a completely solitary character – although there are people in her life, she's not staking everything on that, which he knows too. I think there's a mutual understanding that they're both quite independent individuals. There's support that is provided there but it's not a constant situation.

So it was significant that the story raises their relationship as an issue, but then leaves it in the background?

Yeah. I think if there was a sense that she was just on her own all the time it would put it in a different light. You'd think, 'Well, maybe she's just a bit weird and lonely and that's why she's scrapping around in the mud and the dirt.'

I don't know how well you remember this, but did you start from the friend turning up when you wrote the story or was it always going to be about her clearing?

No, I started with the idea of this barbecue that she's holding out in front of her. I think I found that quite funny.

Just the expression 'disposable barbecue' seemed quite incongruous to the rest of the scene. It stands out as being just a bit shit. I'm surprised she picked it up because she dumps a lot of other artificial stuff in the supermarket.

Yeah, it is quite funny that she's like, 'I don't know what I'm supposed to be doing.' And then she's standing somewhere unusual in the garden when she sees him coming, holding this weird thing that she's trying to work out what to do with. He's not going to look and see her right away because she's never in that spot. And so she can actually look at him while he's expecting her to be probably in the cottage.

And then there's that really wonderful, bizarre sensation that comes from seeing someone who doesn't know you're there because they're expecting you to be somewhere else. Which creates a doubling in you. And that's what I quite liked, because she almost feels as if she's not really where she is; she thinks she actually might be in the cottage and that when he walks in, she will be in there. Though she won't because she's where she is.

And then the carpet's whipped from under her feet because he sees her right away. So then she holds up the barbecue to hide behind; she's like, 'Oh no, it's too soon. You found me too soon. I'm not ready yet.' She thought she was invisible. It's quite funny.

It taps into something that has always interested me. Quite a lot of these ideas stem from my time working in theatre. One of the things that I used to find really aggravating in theatre productions is that a character would come onto the stage talking right away – there's no sense of them coming into being and you gradually discovering them. It's immediate and total and I used to find that too much. Beckett literally covered up parts of people, so you might only get a mouth or the top half of their body, fragmenting them or just making them less total and present and completely established from the off.

So it's interesting that at the beginning of this there was a little bit of play around that. A semi-performance that doesn't quite take.

He disappears quite quickly anyway; he goes off and has a shower, which is strange too. He's like, 'Hello.' And then he goes inside and that's that.

It's not a very conventional look at their interiorities or their relationships. Is this connected to what you said before that you're not that interested in character in the conventional way? It's maybe similar to what you described in Beckett – that they're not a hundred percent present.

Yeah. That's something that interests me in literature as well. It's something you can explore with more nuance than you can in theatre. You get it at the beginning of Proust, when he's waking up in the dark, not quite sure where he is.

I love that. I've always found it a bit too strong when right from the off in a novel or a story, everything's just very established – we know where we are and what it looks like and what these sorts of people are like and what their lives are like – so you get a sense of what the nature of the drama is going to be. It goes back to the objective correlative you mentioned. Setting things up to contextualise the turmoil within. I think it's more interesting when there is a dissonance actually, between a person's situation and how they're feeling. Sometimes out of the blue I'll feel utterly perplexed or on edge and there's no reason for it, there's nothing I can point to. There's really a lot that can't be explained actually.

And does this go back to what you were saying about trying not to work in the old societal frameworks and all the old artifices of what is 'given'?

Possibly, yeah. It doesn't have its origin in anything intellectual or deliberate. It's just how I've always felt about being in the world – that way of thinking about selfhood and individuality and our place in the world and what we should do and where we should get our motivation and direction and values and explanations from and all of that: I always felt it was too externally oriented. The story developed naturally from that.

When I was younger it was a bit confusing and strange and somewhat alienating. As you get older you come across certain philosophies and literary movements and you realise that other people have felt similar things and you understand why certain artistic approaches have developed out of a similar confusion and distrust of those given things.

I wondered if the modernism you're describing, our present literary era has retreated from? Do you feel that few people are keeping to the ideas and the goals and the mode of modernism?

In what way are you thinking that we've retreated from modernism? I don't know. In what way?

I'm thinking of contemporary literature. It seems to be quite 'normal' again. A lot of the old Victorian traditions of just describing things and telling stories. Maybe I'm reading the wrong stuff?

Yeah, you might be. Some of the mainstream stuff I suppose is a bit... I don't know...

So you feel modernism is still vibrant?

I don't know. I mean not in the mainstream so much, but I still think that emphasis on subjective logic is still quite strong in some contemporary work, for sure, and the valuing of direct personal experience, and that capacity to arrange maybe disparate elements of life is still quite strong.

The modernist mode is something that's still being explored and is quite interesting. Particularly in less traditional novels. There's been a lot about fragmentation and fragmented society. There has to be some attempt to respond to that. Although I also have to feel like what I'm living in is cohesive which is where that subjective logic kicks in, because we can't help but create connections between quite disparate elements. That's what T. S. Eliot defined poetry as. We're taking all these things that seem to have no relation, but actually we can – with our imagination if we get really deep into it – we can find ways to make connections in them. And that helps us to live, I suppose, because otherwise it's just living in chaos.

Beckett was a writer who was not afraid to stay with the chaos. He didn't think it was up to the artist to make things clearer, more legible. Then again, there are connections in his work – motifs that recur, memories that resurface, little obsessions – but it's accidental, or unavoidable, it's not intentional, that's not his aim at all. Many of his characters have these peculiarly fastidious systems, the sucking stone and so on, that are perfectly futile and terribly moving, and actually they highlight all that's inexplicable around them, the chaos that looms and presses in.

I feel your writing has a very distinct voice: it feels a bit conversational in tone with its many modifiers, like 'really' and 'very', as though the narrator is finding their way through language to pinpoint what they're describing. I wondered how you came to this writing style? Do the sentences occur to you naturally or is it harder work than that?

At this stage now – ten years on actually from this story – it feels easier to access that. And even then I reached a point where I wasn't having to labour it. But I'd been writing for a long time already by then. Probably about twenty years, since I was very young. And so I was used to that.

I had a relationship with the page and putting my mark on it. And that was something that I'd done for a long time privately. So it was just part of my life in a way; it wasn't daunting. But then creating something for a readership, that did present certain challenges in terms of craft and so on. Realising that you are making something that has to work in particular ways. You have to bring a reader through something. So all of that was the work I suppose: figuring out those things.

How did I negotiate that? Reading, reading a lot. Just seeing what other writers had done. That was a very, very exciting time. Just figuring that all out. The reading is to see what's possible, it just opens something up, you just go, 'Oh, wow.' It's a bit weird – it's a bigger world than you thought; it gets more exciting. It's wonderful. It's like a huge landscape – you're brought into this other part and you think, oh yeah, this is where I hang out. This is great. You feel at home in a way.

And, yeah, I remember reading Witold Gombrowicz and Robert Musil, and Lydia Davis, to find out what doesn't have to be there. What you don't have to do, which was really welcome because there are some very strict ideas about the short story. You're like, 'Oh god, it has to be this long and have these particular elements, and has to do this and that.' You know, the stories that everyone holds up time and again. I remember reading some of them and going, 'I don't really get that. I didn't think that was that great, am I missing something?' And then really feeling, 'Oh god, I'm missing something!' And then finding other stories, other ways, and thinking, 'Oh yeah, that's it.' And it's not that there is no craft in what these other writers are doing – of course there is. I'm thinking about Italo Calvino now, he was very important to me at that time – his book *Six Memos for the Next Millennium* posits a very different way of understanding sentences and language and what they can do. I was deeply impressed by that book, it showed me a whole other way of thinking about what I do and I was so relieved to have come across it.

I was at an author conversation with you recently, when you asked an author what emotion she wrote from. I wondered if there was an emotional spur that got you going or if it was not as defined as that in this particular story?

I don't think there's one particular emotion. But I think for a long time emotion was probably what prompted me to put pen to paper. Although, I think you can get to a place where you move beyond emotion.

I don't know whether or not *Pond* does dip into that place that's beyond emotion. Because emotion is almost like the ultimate experience or the most heightened experience or the most generative – it has a certain potency, a certain *need*. Then you think, well, what can be beyond that? It's interesting to think, is this my emotion? Is this feeling just my feeling? That came about perhaps because of the environment that this narrator lives in, and that sense of age and history of the cottage, the age of the soil, even.

There's that final paragraph that seems to go back in time or back somewhere. It's a bit bizarre. But there's a loosening of the specificity of time and place. We're suddenly elsewhere. Yes. Are we under the ground or what – where are we? We are no longer within the realm of direct, personal, individual experience. Sometimes with emotion you think, well, I'm not the only person who's felt this way; I'm not the only person who has been in this situation which has caused me to feel this way, I'm part of a long line of women, and recognising that is very powerful. It really makes you feel like you are part of something immemorial. And sometimes that feeling can build in me and I probably write from that place – it's deep, but it's not entirely personal.

When you feel like you're part of something larger, could you say what that is? Or is that beyond articulation?

I think it's beyond articulation by its nature. And I think that's what I mean by the end of a story is you getting as far as you can with words and then you realise that that's it. You've come to the limit of it. You're writing towards it because words make things particular. And you're not after a particularity, not ultimately. Words can do an awful lot and are very rich and wonderful. I love what they can do, but there are places where they just can't go, not if you want the thing they have created to have life. That's the paradox. Words can make a thing and they can kill a thing stone dead.

And I think in this story she articulates it under the ground, in the soil: 'I believe that's where I lost my heart.'

I've been reading *The Lonely Voice* by Frank O'Connor recently. It has an epigraph from Pascal, which says, 'The eternal silence of those infinite spaces terrifies me,' which I thought could also be an epigraph to *Pond*. I wondered whether you were also interested in place and how place could trap us, or give us a sense of freedom?

It could have been an epigraph, couldn't it? Actually, space was something I was thinking about a lot. I was reading Bachelard and Tanizaki. It came out of the fact that I was living somewhere that was very old and had a lot of history. Although what do you do with history? How do you live with it or alongside it? We talk about 'living there' and it being 'your place', but can it be your place and still the place that it is at the same time?

It depends upon how notions of home are interpreted. Living in a neoliberalist world where you've got to keep buying stuff has affected it. And also since COVID homes are now multifunctional, they have to be offices and so on. It's reflected in what you see being sold in interior shops and represented in films and stuff. I don't really relate to that because I live on my own and don't have to do a lot of Zoom meetings and that kind of thing. And being on my own made me question, 'Why do I even need a home? Is it just wasted on me? How do I inhabit this space now? I'm not really sure what I'm doing in it.' And that's why the narrator becomes interested in trying to connect with it in a more imaginative, more elemental way.

I guess some of Bachelard was directing me a little bit in some of that. Though his vision of a place of sanctuary is quite utopian to a degree, which doesn't quite tally with my experience of inhabiting, which is precarious a lot of the time. 'How long are you going to be able to live somewhere?' is always the big question.

Tanizaki's *In Praise of Shadows* really made me realise how the home now is functioning more and more as a workplace, with an emphasis on being brightly lit and efficient and connected, it means you must be constantly on and available. And what is that? It's going further and further away from the Bachelardian idea of a home as a place of retreat and privacy and reverie, where you can just be a bit like who you want to be, which might be completely different from who you are out and about. Although that's blurred now. There isn't the person at home and the person out and about. The public and the private have had to merge. And what does that do, I wonder, to your interior space?

The reader can feel the impressions of these quite intellectual ideas, like a brass rubbing, but are they present in your mind when you're writing?

I did a lot of reading and thinking for a long time. And then, when it comes to writing, I'm not thinking about those things anymore. It's like, years ago when I was in a play – *Miss Julie* – we did a first dress rehearsal and afterwards the director said to me, 'Look, you can forget everything we've done in rehearsal now.' I said, 'What do you mean?' He said, 'You've done the work, you have it. Trust that you have it and don't give it a second thought now – just go on and be.' And I was like, 'Oh yeah, okay, I totally get what you mean. Sure.' So that's what happens, you let go of it; you don't refer back to it or strive for it. You just know it's absolutely and integrally there and is going to come out in whatever you do.

I thought of that final fragmentary section when you talk about a movement away from the particular. I wondered when you read it now, how you feel about that part?

Yeah, I like it. It annoys me a bit because I haven't really been able to do anything quite like that since. I'd like to have stayed in that mode but that was the extent of whatever that was. That part was written in one go and, to be honest, I probably wrote it before I wrote the story. And then I just put it on the end.

Could you say why?

I have things, and I think, what am I ever going to do with that? It's just a short thing that comes quite quickly. And then maybe months or years later, I'll see a place for it. And I'll go, 'That's great. That's where it goes. That's where it needs to go.'

I don't know at what point I knew, but I just saw that this piece had been writing towards that much earlier fragment. Well, that's overstating it a bit. But they belonged to the same broken pot if you like.

Did you learn anything, maybe if not from the writing of this story, then actually from the process of writing *Pond*? Was there something that shaped you or made you the writer you are now?

Yeah. I suppose it's like with any first book, you get some understanding of just what it is you want to do. I'm still realising what kind of writer I am, which is useful, because then you don't get annoyed with yourself for not doing certain things. Then you can say, 'Well, actually, I'm not that writer anyway, so there's no point getting annoyed with myself.'

So it told me a lot about what I value, what interests me. And I don't look back on the story, or the book, and cringe. I find it quite useful, to go back and look at it. I've got a lot of fondness for it. It reminds me that I have to just keep coming back to nothing in a way, just keep returning to nothing. And then I have certain touchstones around that nothing. It's difficult to describe what it shows you, because in a way it's like looking into black water. It's a weird feeling. You are confronted with something strange and utterly familiar.

The Bunker

by Mark Haddon

Nadine was returning from a day shift at the hospital when it happened for the first time. A fug of sweat and cigarettes and damp coats on the top deck of a number 23, then a windy walk high over the river on that fine white rainbow of cast iron, stopping at the central point as she always did, to lean over the railings and pretend for a few moments that she was airborne like the ravens that played out there in the updraught. A few blessed moments with no people making demands of her before she returned home to the flat, Edith handed Bennie over and she was at someone's beck and call again. A hundred feet below, a small boat puttered upstream on the dirty, moss-green tide. She glanced at her watch and felt a stab of guilt. Time to go.

Past the laundrette, the bookies and the Trawlerman, then dipping into the Co-operative for a *Telegraph* and the pint of milk her mother-in-law would almost certainly have forgotten to buy.

She crossed the cool, tiled hall of the Mansions and stepped into the lift. A ring of light appeared around her fingertip as she pressed the button for the fifth floor. The doors closed, the slack in the cable was taken up and she rose through the building.

Halfway between the second and third floors she tasted something bitter at the back of her throat. Her legs became unsteady and she had to grip the metal rail to hold herself upright. The brushed steel of the lift's wall, the emergency sign, her own hands, none of them seemed real. There was a loud, sparking crackle and the world shrank to a single bright point, like a television screen being turned off. She floated briefly in absolute darkness, then light and noise flooded back and she was standing, not in the lift, but at the side of a busy road looking at a row of dirty red-brick houses in the rain. The street was full of people, running, shouting, crying. She recognised none of the buildings. She had never been here before. One woman simply stood and stared into the distance, dropped bags of shopping at her feet, a tin of Ambrosia creamed rice rolling into the gutter through spilt flour turning milky on the wet pavement. A white and sky-blue panda car screeched to a halt at the kerb beside her and a policeman got out. 'Nadine Pullman?'

She was too shocked to reply, shocked that she was visible, shocked that someone knew her name, that she was not just looking at this scene but a part of it.

'Get in.' She didn't move. 'I'm serving you with a B47 notice, now sodding well get into the car or I swear by Almighty God...' She got into the car. The policeman jumped back into the driving seat and gunned the engine.

A woman in an olive gaberdine grabbed the wing mirror and screamed for help. They roared away from the kerb and she tumbled backwards, holding the ripped-off mirror in her hands.

The car tilted and squealed round the corners. A zigzagging Bedford truck came close to hitting them.

'What's happening?' It was her voice but it wasn't her voice. 'What the bloody hell do you think is happening?'

They crested a hill and skidded into a small lane. 'Out!' He left the key in the ignition. Three men were running up a concrete staircase built into a high grass bank. One of them was wearing a butcher's apron. She could hear sirens. 'Move!' She tripped and lost a shoe. The policeman grabbed her arm and dragged her up the steps, scraping her ankles and ripping her stockings. He pulled her through a thick double door into a crowded entryway, then let her drop. A man and a woman ran up the steps behind them, waving cream certificates with red seals. A bald man in spectacles barked, 'Last two!' and as they crossed the threshold he swung the heavy door shut and it rang like a gong. He locked it with quarter-turns of the levers at its four corners.

There was another sparking crackle, everything shrank to a similar bright point, and after a few moments of darkness Nadine found herself lying on the floor of the lift. How long had she been away? Seconds? Minutes? The door was open and Mr Kentridge from flat 17 was staring down at her. 'Are you unwell, Mrs Pullman?'

She got slowly to her feet, explaining that it was her time of the month and that this sometimes made her sick and light-headed. 'I need to go and sit down.'

He held up his hands, not wanting to continue a conversation on this subject. She walked to the door of the flat, steadying herself against the wall, then turned to make sure that he had entered the lift and descended.

Martin's mother was asleep on the yellow sofa, eyes closed, head resting against the antimacassar. Bennie was dozing in her lap, thumb in his mouth. She wanted a cup of tea but didn't trust her shaking hands with the kettle, the matches and the gas. Instead she opened the window and lit a Kensitas. The sun was starting to go down and lights were coming on, the dark buildings turning slowly into advent calendars.

The panic in the streets, the green metal door, the airlock. There was no doubt about it. Mr Kentridge had suspected nothing, that was some consolation. She massaged her forehead as if the problem were merely a headache. From miles away she heard the sad song of a ferry clearing the harbour. That unforgettable vision of her uncle's final minutes, so clear she forgot sometimes that she had not witnessed them with her own eyes, the neighbours dragging him out of the cottage and into the little strip of woodland beside the railway. She had seen him a couple of days before the end, raving about sinks and fire orders and black holes. Her aunt's desperate desire to save him warring with the knowledge that the fight was already lost. 'There's nothing more that we can do, Nadine. Please. We need to get away from here.' Hoping that the doctors would reach him first. Though who knew which fate was worse.

'Mummy... ?' Bennie was waking.

They said that if you'd been there once then you were lost. But who would be foolish enough to broadcast their good luck if they had visited the other world and come back merely scorched?

'Mummy... ?'

She cooked a lamb and carrot stew. She remembered and forgot and remembered, every occasion a jug of iced water down her spine. Edith complained about her hip. She heard herself being sympathetic and was surprised at the skill with which she dissembled. Bennie was teething. She rubbed clove oil on his gums. What would happen to him? Not just the absence of a mother but the taint of having had this mother in particular.

Martin returned just after seven. Nadine hoped he would sense her distress but he was preoccupied with some difficulty at the workshop involving a three-piece suite and an unpaid bill. After supper Martin played snap and piggybacks with Bennie, then put him to bed. The adults then listened to Joan Sutherland on the radio.

She lay in bed unable to sleep, Martin dead to the world beside her. So gentle for such a big man. She'd seen him lift a car so that the wheel could be changed. They'd met at a coffee concert in the Wellesley Room, Martin absurd in his undersized suit. Haydn's 'Sunrise' before the interval, Beethoven's 'Grosse Fuge' after. Two brilliant violins poorly served. He could protect her. She had thought it before they'd even spoken.

She had two fathers. One was sober, one was drunk. The first became the second when the sun went down. The beatings weren't the worst. It was the waiting in between which ate away at her. She brought Martin home for tea and Martin held her father's eye for the most uncomfortable ten seconds of her life and her father never touched her again. But now? This wasn't a drunken father. This wasn't a flat tyre and a missing jack.

Above her in the gloom the plaster cornices turned slowly monstrous.

Three uneventful days encouraged the hope that she'd had a very narrow escape, the burden of her terrible secret growing slowly lighter as she changed dressings and emptied bedpans. The man who had fallen from the scaffolding two months earlier took his first steps and they threw a party.

On the fourth day she was sitting on one of the benches outside the staff canteen, next to the blackthorn hedge which half-hid the boiler plant. She was eating the mustard and potted meat sandwich she had made that morning and wrapped in greaseproof paper so that she could carry it in her handbag. Again, the bitter taste, the sparking crackle, the darkness and, suddenly, she was holding an exercise book bearing a black crown and the words *AWDREY LOG: Supplied for the Public Service HMSO Code 28-616*. She could smell sweat and human excrement. Mounted on the wall to her right was a grid of tiny wooden boxes, the kind a school librarian might use for storing index cards. One was labelled *DEAD*, another *CONFIRMED*.

Three men in pigeon-grey military jackets were leaning over a broad table. Behind them was a wall of Perspex on which a big map of the country had been gridded and subdivided. She was in a room smaller than half a tennis court. It had no windows. One of the men looked up. His stubble and his red eyes suggested that he had neither slept nor shaved for several days. 'Well... ?'

'Two new blasts. Blast one: fifty miles, bearing a hundred and fifty two degrees.' The words were coming out of her mouth but she had no idea what they meant. 'Six to eight megatons. RAF Scampton.' 'Dear God,' said the man. 'And the second blast... ?'

'The second...' Her mind was blank.

'For Christ's sake, we do not have all day.'

His colleague turned to him, a gangly man with a wizard's beard who was clearly not used to wearing a uniform. 'I fear that we have all the time in the world.'

'Miss Pullman.' The red-eyed man turned back to Nadine. 'A little kindness would not go amiss,' said the bearded man.

'Miss Pullman –' the red-eyed man ignored his colleague –'there is limited air. There is limited water. You have a job to do and that is the only reason you are here. Illness is not an option. Mental collapse is not an option.'

The sparking crackle sounded again and after a short period of darkness she was lying on her back staring up at a blue sky, the blackthorn bush and two worried people gazing down at her. Dr Cairns offered a hand to ease her to her feet. Sister Collins guided her to the bench. Cold sweat and a deep churn in her guts. 'Nurse Catterick, fetch Nurse Pullman a glass of cold water.'

It was only a matter of time now. Her friends and colleagues wouldn't turn her in, but gossip spread and it only took one person who valued their safety above your life. Dr Peterson had been taken away in a black van, Nurse

Nimitz had been taken away, the handsome Trinidadian man with sickle cell had been taken away...

She went home early, bright autumn sun falling on a world to which she no longer belonged. There was a fair in Queen's Gardens, a chained baby elephant in a nest of straw, painted horses turning, a jaunty pipe organ and the smell of burnt sugar.

She had no idea what to expect from this point on. They had wiped her uncle from the family record, as if ignorance were a form of protection, and what she heard elsewhere was a tangle of gossip, half-truth and scaremongering. Some said that it was contagious insanity, others that these were echoes of past events, others that they were premonitions of events still to come. The end of the world, some whispered.

There were no articles in the papers. It was not discussed on the radio or the television. Her lack of interest seemed shameful in retrospect. Not once had she put herself in these shoes. So much suffering and her only thought had been relief that it was happening to someone else.

She had Bennie on her knee when it happened for a third time. 'This is the way the ladies ride. Clip-clop, clip-clop...' Edith had retreated to her room with *The Grand Sophy* and a mug of cocoa which might or might not have contained a shot of Bowmore, and Bennie was hungry for some of the riotousness that Edith's age and hip were making increasingly impossible. 'This is the way the gentlemen ride...'

It was quicker this time, more like a doorway than a journey. No bitter taste, just a rapid crackle, Bennie falling backwards out of her grasp, and she was waking from a shallow sleep in a cramped dormitory of eight bunks. Half-submarine, half-boarding school. Her skin was sticky, her hair lank. A woman in uniform was waiting to take her place under the dirty sheet and khaki blanket. The words *Royal Observer Corps* curved over a red aeroplane on her shoulder. Nadine looked down and saw that she had been sleeping in an identical grey uniform. Fifteen other women were climbing out of bed. Fifteen different women were waiting to take their places.

Someone was singing 'Walking Back to Happiness'.

'For God's sake, Rita. Can it, will you.'

'Girls, girls...'

The women crossed the corridor and entered the room she recognised from the last time. The strip lights, the Perspex wall maps. She was the tail of the crocodile. The red-eyed man stepped in front of her and closed the door so that they were alone in the corridor. The chug of machinery somewhere and the faint odour of diesel fumes. She could see now that there was a triangle of waxy flesh on his chin where no stubble grew. He had been burnt as a child, perhaps.

'I need to know one thing and one thing only.'

'What's that?'

'Can you do your job?'

She closed her eyes and looked into her mind and saw fragments of something which had broken or fallen apart... a boiler suit made of white cotton... the EM wave and the optical wave... the sound of someone weeping at the end of a phone line...

'Miss Pullman... ?'

She felt a rising panic and a painful yearning to be somewhere safe with no responsibilities. Her knees gave way and she slid down the wall until she was sitting on the scratchy grey carpet, sobbing. 'I think that's a fairly conclusive "no".'

Martin sat in the rocking chair beside the bed. She had been away for longer this time.

'Where's Bennie... ?'

'He bumped his head. My mother has taken him to the fair. Toffee apple and candyfloss. He will be royally sick by the time he gets home.'

'I should have told you earlier.'

He cupped her cheek in his hands and shook his head. Was he saying goodbye? Were the doctors drumming their fingers in the living room, giving the two of them a final few moments' grace? Under the fear was a relief she had not expected.

'We're going to see an exorcist.'

Were it not for the steady confidence of his gaze she might have questioned his sanity. She knew about exorcists only through fourth-hand stories. She had always assumed that they were figments of desperate imaginations.

'There are things I have never told you.' He got to his feet. 'Things you were safer not knowing.' He handed her the black duffel coat he had laid over the arm of the chair. 'Put this on. We have a long, cold walk ahead of us.'

They slipped into an alleyway off Weaver's Lane, then cut across the graveyard of St Saviour's. Martin was a big man who attracted attention but the few people who passed them in the darkened streets seemed not to notice them. Only a dog was disturbed by their presence, growling at the end of its chain, hackles up and head down. It was the strangeness of the evening, perhaps, or her growing detachment from her own life, but she felt as if she were traversing a city which was almost but not quite identical to the one in which she lived.

He said, 'I told you sometimes that I would be working late. It was not always true.' He said, 'I've never talked about my sister. We lost her. I promised I would never lose anyone again.' He said, 'I've done this for nineteen other people. I hoped I'd never have to do it for you.'

They were heading downhill towards the docks. Fish and marine oil on the wind. The lights of the Raleigh still blazed, its patrons blurry behind dripping, foggy glass. They walked through a mazy canyon of warehouses. A big rat trotted casually past like a tiny insurance clerk late for the office. A misty smudge of moon lit their way. They turned a corner and the moon was swallowed by a double-funnelled steamer in red and cream, roped to the quayside and portholed on three decks from stem to stern.

Martin led her to the foot of a cast-iron fire escape which rose steeply to a door between two dirty, lit windows which might have been the eyes of a harbourmaster's office were it not for the lack of signage. They mounted the ringing steps.

The exorcist was a plump, forgettable woman whose ivy-green cardigan was fastened by walnut-brown toggles. She greeted Martin with the wordless nod one gave to a colleague. 'So this is Nadine.'

There was a Rolodex. There was a vase of dying irises. There was a framed reproduction of Bruegel's *Fall of Icarus*, the glass cracked at the corner. A bagatelle board leaning against a wall would have seemed bizarre on any other day. Nadine took the empty armchair.

'I'm afraid we have no time for pleasantries.' The woman was steelier than she appeared. 'You have to trust me completely and you must do exactly as I say. There is no alternative.' Nadine glanced round and Martin nodded his assent. 'The next time you cross over I will be waiting for you on the other side. We will not mention this meeting. We will not talk of Martin or your son. We will not talk of this world. Do you understand?' The woman leant forwards and Nadine saw a charm bracelet slip from the cuff of her cardigan, a silver chain from which hung a little silver crow, a little silver moon and a little silver hammer.

'I understand.'

'I will try hard to find you a way home. I cannot tell you in advance what it will be. I can only tell you that I have not failed yet.' Somewhere nearby the bell of a mariner's chapel tolled twice. 'I must go. I have difficult work to do.' The exorcist stood slowly. She seemed to be in some pain. 'When you next see me I will be changed.'

She took a macramé shoulder bag and a dark blue cagoule from the back of the chair. 'Get some rest.' Then she was gone.

Martin sat on the arm of the chair and held her. She had many questions, but to ask any of them would open the door of the aircraft mid-flight. Better not to see how far she had to fall. She wanted more than anything to be with Bennie.

'Remember that first long walk we took?' Martin sandwiched her tiny hand between his great paws. 'Near Minehead?' A thundercloud had risen over Selworthy Beacon and the sunshine was replaced suddenly by a slate sky and hail like conkers. They ran hand in hand for a pillbox where they startled the sleeping, ownerless spaniel who would later accompany them for the remainder of the walk. 'Let's take it again...'

She leant her head against the dependable mass of him. 'OK.'

'So... I picked you up from your parents' house. It was half-past nine in the morning. You were wearing the orange skirt with the yellow circles...'

An hour, two hours... She slept and woke and did not recognise her surroundings and was briefly terrified until she saw Martin, only to succumb to a different fear when she remembered why she was here with the dying irises and the bagatelle board. She slept again and woke and drank a glass of tepid water from the pitcher on the desk, and was standing at the window watching faint smudges of pumpkin-coloured light pick out the cranes and the hulks at anchor when she left the world for the final time.

No taste, no noise, no darkness. Instantly she was sitting at a Formica-topped table in a canteen. On the far side of the table was the gangly, bearded man. Behind him sat a uniformed woman Nadine did not recognise. She had a lazy eye and black, black hair. There was a serving hatch and the rank perfume of boiled vegetables. She looked around for the exorcist but there was no one else in the room. The Formica had unglued itself from the chipboard at the table's corner.

'I apologise for Major Pine's graceless behaviour. He is correct, but there are many different ways of being correct.' She could hear now that the man's accent was a soft, lowland Scots. 'In better times you would have been cared for.' He sighed. 'But in better times our lives would not depend on a man like Major Pine.'

His female colleague sat back and said nothing, as if she were supervising the man's training.

He cleared his throat and read from the sheaf of stapled papers. 'You signed documents during your training to the effect that if, on active service with ROC Group Number Twenty, you became incapacitated either physically or mentally...' He dropped the paper. '...and some more turgid bureaucratic nonsense I won't bore you with.' He rubbed his eyes. 'They want you to sign a piece of paper. Can you believe that? Because the last man in the world will be some prig from Whitehall trudging across the scorched wasteland checking paperwork.' The woman seemed neither surprised nor affronted by the diatribe. He pushed a pamphlet across the table. 'Predictably, they provide a helpful guide to the situation.'

Expulsion: A Guide to Short Term Survival. She flipped through the pages. *Root vegetables from allotments and gardens may provide another source of relatively uncontaminated food...* There was a diagram showing how to kill a poorly drawn dog, though whether for protection or consumption it was not immediately clear. She was transfixed by the backs of the hands that were and weren't hers, the dirt under the nails, the faint blue of returning blood. They were so real. She had never heard anyone speak about how utterly convincing it all was.

'You know as much as anyone.' The man shrugged. 'Leeds has gone. Manchester has gone. The destruction is widespread from Holy Loch south. In other circumstances I would pray for God to go with you, but my faith in the old chap has been somewhat undermined of late.' He stood up and pushed his chair back under the table, the legs screeching on the lino. 'I wish you a strong wind off the North Sea and a cache of tinned beans.' He gestured towards the door. 'Let's get this ghastly business over with.'

The woman followed them into the corridor. Where was the exorcist? Nadine was increasingly certain that something had gone wrong. The man stood aside so that Nadine could take the stairs first. She felt sick. None of this was real. She had to remember that.

The man waited for a few seconds, then said, 'I would much rather that this passed off without any unpleasantness.'

She climbed to the concrete landing where she had entered the building that first time. A big cream hatch stood open revealing an airlock not much larger than a toilet cubicle, rubber seals, pressure gauges and a red warning light in a sturdy wire cage. The far wall was a sealed, identical hatch. And beyond that?

'It will be cold outside.' The black-haired woman held out a dark duffel coat, identical to the one Nadine had worn for the long walk earlier that evening, but older and dirtier with a skirl of torn lining dangling below the hem. Worlds slid over one another, like a cathedral reflected in a café window, like the beach and the christening on the same photograph.

And then she saw them, in the shadow of the woman's military cuff, a crow, a moon, a hammer. 'Thank you.'

The man stared hard at the wall over Nadine's shoulder, unwilling to meet her eye. She stepped into the airlock. She was not going to turn round. She was not going to treat him like a real person. She focused instead on a long cream-coloured drip where a painter had overloaded his brush. Were these the echoes of some vanished world? Was this the future? It seemed inconceivable that her own mind could conjure a universe so rich in detail.

The man said, 'I wish you luck,' the hinges squeaked and, with a soft kiss, seal met seal. There were four muffled clangs as the locks were turned on the landing, then nothing, only the sound of her breathing in the steel chamber.

She closed her eyes and pictured herself unconscious in the armchair in that little room, Martin at the window waiting for her to be returned to him. Outside, dockers yelled and busy tugboats worked at the jigsaw puzzle of the big freighters. Bananas and coal and coffee. Bennie would surely be awake now, wanting to know where she was.

Nadine opened her eyes. There was a dirty grille at waist height. There was an abandoned pair of black wellington boots. There was a waste bin bearing the label *Contaminated Overalls Only*. In what way was a duffel coat meant to help? Had she deceived herself? Had she seen what she wanted to see in the glitter of some other jewellery?

The red light came on and began to turn. Then the alarm went off, stupidly loud in such a small space. She covered her ears. Five, six seconds? The alarm stopped and the red light went out. She took her hands from her ears and heard the dull hiss of air pressures equalising. The big door unlocked itself and let in a thin slice of grey light and a sweet, charred smell which raised the hairs on the back of her neck. She put the duffel coat on for the small comfort it offered and carefully opened the door.

The panda car was burnt out, the paint black and blistered. Orange rust was already eating away at the unprotected metal, the tyres were gone, the glass was gone. There were no windows in any of the buildings. Many walls had fallen. Roofs were shipwrecks of black timbers. A thick, unwashed fog hid the far side of the park across the road. Every patch of grass was dead. She walked down the steps. Two silhouettes on a nearby wall looked like the shadows of children if children could leave shadows behind. The airlock bumped softly shut behind her. She listened. It was the kind of silence she had only ever heard on a still day in the mountains.

A burnt dog lay beside the burnt car.

There was movement in the corner of her eye. She turned and saw a tramp standing at the lane's dead end, holding the hand of a girl of seven or eight. Their faces were soiled. He wore three dirty coats and carried a crowbar. There was an open wound on the girl's cheek.

'Oi! Lady!'

The woman had been right. The air was bitterly cold. She slipped her hands into the pockets of the duffel coat. There was something hard and heavy in the right-hand side. She lifted out a tarnished, snub-nosed pistol. The words *Webley & Scott Ltd, London & Birmingham* were stamped into the side of a fat, square stock. The trigger guard was a primitive hoop and the hammer looked like a sardine key. A gentle squeeze of the trigger showed that the machinery was oiled and ready.

'You were in that bloody bunker, weren't you!' The man was limping towards her, dragging the girl behind him.

'You did this!' He swung the crowbar around, indicating the fallen walls, the dead grass. 'You people did this!'

Suddenly she understood. 'You have to trust me completely.' Nothing had gone wrong. The exorcist had found her a way home. 'Are you listening to me, lady?'

She put the barrel of the gun into her mouth and bit the metal hard to hold it steady.

Running a Punch and Judy Show:
Mark Haddon on 'The Bunker'

Mark Haddon is the author of many novels for adults and children, and of two books of short stories. He has won the Whitbread Award, the Guardian Children's Fiction Prize, and a Commonwealth Writers' Prize for his work.

I asked Mark about how he wanted to write the two worlds in 'The Bunker', and what effects he was interested in.

I read that this story started from a sense of place, from your experience of visiting a real bunker. How did this starting point affect the writing and direction of the story?

It was a commission from English Heritage who were producing a collection of ghost stories. I usually avoid commissions like the plague. I was sent to a boarding school as a teenager – 'a kind of open prison with good cultural facilities' was the phrase I once used in an interview and I'm sticking with it – and I've had a profound dislike of being told what to do ever since. As a consequence I've only ever taken on commissions when I have been able to subvert them somehow.

In this case, I ran through the English Heritage catalogue and found their most atypical property, the York Cold War Bunker. Turning it over in my mind I thought it would provide the ideal setting for a story that both was and wasn't a ghost story.

The bunker was haunting, very haunting indeed, and historically much more immediate than almost anything else English Heritage owns – It's not in aspic yet, and still feels like living history.

How did your visit inspire you to get a first glimmer of the story?

Firstly, it was the experience of the place itself. The claustrophobia, the military paraphernalia, that terrifying future we were preparing for. I took lots of photographs and scribbled in my notebook. Not just to get a sense of what would happen if there was a nuclear attack to the north of England (which is where the Royal Observer Corps would watch it unfold) but to gather a collection of what I thought would be the most flavoursome details.

Research itself doesn't make things 'real'. Technically correct descriptions are often not very believable on account of being rather dull, I think readers are convinced by the skill and verve of the writing. You only need to get a few details to jump off the page to make the whole story feel authentic, so for me research is about cherry-picking the best of these, the ones that will snag the readers' imaginations.

The second place the story came from was the old Daoist story by Zhuangzi, about a philosopher who doesn't know whether he's a philosopher dreaming of being a butterfly, or a butterfly dreaming of being a philosopher. Though, of course, that story pulls its punches when it declares from the off that he's a philosopher, which means there's no existential horror. Real horror would have come from flipping between those two realities without knowing which is which. That has always been a theme for me: can you be pulled into a story so far that you don't know which is real, this or the 'life' you left behind? That queasy toggle between two worlds, both of which might be real.

It's been a perennial fascination for me, and only after recently writing a memoir did I realise it wasn't simply a fascination with an abstract idea, but stems in large part from my childhood, from that boarding school – I have a vivid memory of being at home and thinking, 'I hate this. I need to escape back to school again' and then going back to school and thinking, 'Shit, no, *this* is the nightmare'. Rinse and repeat.

So after coming back from the bunker with these notes and photographs, did you have the sense of this duality framework already?

Yes, I guess that trope, the porous border between two alternative worlds is always there waiting at the back of my mind for a story to dramatise it.

Very early on I also had the opening image of a character walking across a bridge early in the morning and looking down on a river. And once I'd placed her there, filling in the rest of her life was relatively easy. Physical space is very important to me in fiction. I can describe the location of every scene in every story I've ever written even if it's not there on the page. The layout of the room, the floor plan of the building, the view from the window. My father was an architect and I think I've inherited his way of picturing the world. I feel a profound sense of something missing when I read a work that doesn't locate its scenes like this. I think, 'Give me a map, show me the furniture, describe the fittings.' For me, fiction needs that solid anchoring.

Which plays against the very disorienting world of a story – the environs are very concrete but the world beyond is misty and unreliable.

Yes, if you have hammered the physical world down, if you've made it *really* real, that gives you the freedom to be more fantastical elsewhere.

And is being fantastical something you feel freer to do in a short story?

I feel freer to do everything in a short story because the risks are smaller. You're not going to spend two years filling the wastepaper basket if it goes wrong. You might go down a cul de sac for a couple of months but it's nowhere near as painful.

The pull of the fantastical has grown for me over the decades. I've had more than my fill of stories about the lives of university-educated middle class white people like myself. Thankfully they're being pushed more towards the margins of the big buffet table of fiction. From where I'm sitting, I see far more narratives about varied and diverse lives, and more fiction from other languages and other cultures. And that's all good. But when it comes to my own fiction it means I have to make an effort to get away from that old-fashioned default of naturalistic stories about people like me.

I sometimes imagine a three-dimensional space with that old-fashioned default at its origin. My job is to find some route away from that origin. It might be into the future with science fiction or speculative fiction, it might involve changing history, it might involve changing physics and biology, it might involve messing with the mechanisms of fiction itself, but there has to be some way you can pull away from that centre. Because that centre is dying.

So amongst other things, is it a political decision who to represent and how to represent?

It *is* political but it also comes from the gut. I find myself bored and annoyed when I read about people who have a Boden catalogue on the coffee table.

With that opening image, could you say why the bird's eye view is powerful for you?

I've thought about this a lot and believe it might be something universal about the view children have of the world, something most of us carry through into adulthood. Almost everyone knows the delight of being on a roof or up a tree or at a high window and looking down. It's a combination of seeing everything without being easily seen yourself, it's about being safe but knowing what everyone else is up to. I suspect it goes bone deep, DNA deep. Perhaps it's no more than me still feeling that childhood preference for looking down from a safe hiding place.

Yes, I suppose in a childhood where you rarely have any control, it's a moment of godlikeness?

Yeah, I would suggest that certainly in this country the majority of older adults would have good memories of being at the top of a climbing frame or even in a treehouse – a treehouse was pretty much the top toy of the 1960s or 70s.

Although, now I think about it, what strikes me is that there's an opposite idea in this story, which is the slightly more niche childhood pleasure of being safely tucked away underground. That love of tunnels, cellars, holes – I was writing recently about a book I loved in my childhood called *Diggy Takes His Pick* which begins with an image of a mole waking up underground in a cottage-like cave, with a chequered bedspread and a little candle by the bed. Somehow that potent image has stayed with me ever since.

I'm thinking on my feet here but I realise now that there's two antithetical images underpinning *The Bunker*, alongside the contrast between the two worlds: on the one hand the freedom to look down, in Nadine's life above ground; and, on the other, the security of living underground, which of course becomes very very unsafe, a trap in fact. Being buried is also one of the worst kinds of nightmare.

Thinking about this image of the bunker made me really appreciate the great twentieth-century fear of looming nuclear war. Nowadays we're mostly anxious about the environmental crisis and have forgotten how close we came to nuclear war. Was there something you wanted to show about that threat?

I was born during the Cuban missile crisis and grew up in its long shadow. The difference between the environmental crisis now and the nuclear crisis then is that you and I in the UK are relatively well off and that wealth will protect most of us in the short term. It's the poor who will suffer – who *are* suffering. With nuclear war there was no escape. It was a great leveller. We might all be the person with hideous tumours and skin peeling off as the sky goes black.

So it was no accident that out of all the English Heritage properties you went for the bunker?

Yes, it felt charged.

Once you had the sense of the framework, how much were you able to follow your nose and how much were you fulfilling a previously-set plan?

I had a loose overall plan which was a kind of receptacle, an idea of a curse that fell upon some people that meant they slipped between a first bright world into the other nightmarish world. Within that framework, I followed my nose.

One of my guiding principles when I write is not to explain too much. Just hint. It's the thing that sinks so many films and TV shows – exposition. Hint enough that people can work out that there is this curse of slippage – and then just move around it and concentrate on things like ice creams, fairgrounds, the sound of ships' horns.

I tell writers the urge to explain is the opposite to the urge to narrate. It means we participate less in the story because the writer hasn't got a sense of us.

And also it's far more pleasing as a reader to be mystified rather than patronised. I'd much prefer to be treated as more intelligent than I am than less intelligent than I am.

Because you didn't explain, I was all the more intrigued when I found that my initial sense of a 'safe' world and 'dangerous' world became twisted and it appeared there was a threat in both of them. Was that something you came to or something you started with?

I have to make characters suffer in order to write the sort of short story I like. I'm less interested in those tangential mood-based minimal melancholic stories. I want actual stuff to happen. I want significant events. I want – to use that terrible word – an arc. And for a proper arc you need bad stuff to happen to people. That's the fuel that gets the whole thing off the runway. I don't like confrontation in real life but you have to treat people badly on the page. You have to light a fire under them.

You've got to dramatise it?
Yes.

In these unexplained parts, did *you* have a sense of the metaphysics of the two worlds that you weren't explaining to us?

I don't know anything beyond the story. I think that's important. You have to see it from the reader's point of view. There's no point building a whole world then hiding parts of it. You have to create an experience which allows for many possibilities in the reader's mind.

For me the place where this happened most frequently – and this was a real education – was the end of the *Curious Incident of the Dog in the Night-time*. I had lots of readers who wanted to know what happened after the end of the book, and I would reply – trying not to crush readers' hopes, particularly the younger ones: 'It's a book. It contains everything I know about those characters and that situation.'

Yes, there's lots of people who like things to be resolved, and I think the short story reader is better at operating without resolution.

I'd go further than that. An ideal reaction for me is that any number of people should be able to read the same story and go away and disagree profoundly about it and all have had equally valid and enjoyable experiences.

You did that with such poise in this story that I've read it a few times and disagree with myself. There's one sentence I've read in different ways: 'And that was the last time she went into that world' – it could be her salvation, it could also be something more terrible. How was it creating these ambiguities?

There's a real sensual pleasure in having written something like that, it's analogous to those lines that are funny *and* painful.

Writing it, you have a sense of, 'Yes, I've got it – the thing is there!'

What would you say that 'thing' is?

It's the ambiguity. It's being halfway through the veil, between one side and the other. The profound experience of reading – when it's good – and writing – when you get there – is that of hovering on the border of the real and the imagined. On some level all good writing is *about* writing. It's about our ability to conjure a world, about the fact that you're just reading inky hieroglyphs that become transparent and lead you elsewhere.

I think that 'the thing' is much more evident in theatre. It's lovely being swept away but my most treasured moments in the theatre are when I am both fully inside the story yet simultaneously aware of its artifice. Your belief is suspended but you're also celebrating that fact.

In Peter Brook's *Mahabharata* there's a scene where someone fires an arrow, and you see the arrow carried very slowly across the stage by an actor. You're both there in the scene and also enjoying that it's being made up. It's the real and the artificial at the same time. A doubleness.

Many readers might have wanted to see the rules governing the two worlds, would have looked for the satisfaction in knowing beforehand, for example, that her attempt to get free would need an exorcist. You didn't want to add that information in the story?

No – it's partly to do with the necessary limitations of prose. I enjoy lo-fi sci-fi fantasy on film and TV. It's relatively easy to do it on TV because there's a lot of parallel processing going on.

While you have the dialogue and the acting in the foreground, the world-building can be done in the background. You can do the architecture and the landscaping simply by increasing the bandwidth.

But writing is always only one channel; you're reading a single word at a time, a single sentence at a time. Which means that every time you do exposition, there's something else you're not doing – and that has a cost. It's one of the reasons why I seldom really enjoy fantasy or detective fiction on the page, because there's so much business that needs to be done and that business takes time away from what I really love in fiction, which is the exquisiteness of the instrument of language being played well.

So for the reason of simple economics – the economics of the time you've got with the reader, the economics of the limited number of words on a page – you need to be as lean as you can be in creating another world. A really good example of that is in Olga Ravn's *The Employees* – nothing is explained there, and it works gloriously. It started out as a description of sculptures in an exhibition and it manages to generate an entire universe, as much by what it doesn't say as what it says.

And to achieve this economy of prose, do you get it straight away in the writing, or is this something that comes in the editing?

I think I'm an okay writer but a really good editor. So much depends on the confidence the reader feels in your voice. You can take a reader anywhere as long as they trust you. I keep flipping hats, from being the writer to being a reader and thinking, 'Does that feel right? Is that giving me pleasure? Does that feel in-tune?'

It's not a million miles away from being a good liar. I'm a *very* good liar if I need to be. My wife tells me I can lie with creepy efficiency. When she lies she has to give off some signal because she knows on some level that God is watching, whereas I know that if I lie, I'm lying with good reason and I have to get it right. And you get it right by sticking as near to the truth as possible – that's the golden rule of lying. And that applies to fiction as well. Stick as near to the real as possible.

Simon Stephens, who adapted *The Curious Incident* for the stage, told me about one scene in a play of his, when someone buys a gun. He said, 'I got all the details on how you buy a gun exactly right. I knew once I'd got that right, the audience would trust me.' You need that one very firm anchor.

I found the way you fixed this anchor in this story is very resonant. The details we zoomed in on – the patch on the major's chin, the recurrence of dogs, amongst others – had the effect of making it feel slightly hyper-realistic, as if we were looking too closely at these details. Were you doing these intentionally?

It's something I'm doing all the time. It's how I look at the world.

It's your lying?

It's my lying. But also my listening and looking. I'm a noticer. I suspect most writers are. And one of the reasons why we go to fiction is to share a kind of intense noticing that we don't do ourselves. We want to stand next to that writer and be made to slow down and look at the world with more care and more focus than we usually do. There's something about the simple pleasure of that noticing, of individual things being highlighted and framed.

And in 'The Bunker', can you say why *these* details? Are these elements that are instinctively interesting to you, or are they pieces of a jigsaw puzzle?

They are just part of the vast sack of stuff that I fill as I go around the world. I don't keep a notebook. These images all exist somewhere in the back of my head. And I like the lack of notebook because it means I only write about the things that have really stuck with me. For example, in both of these worlds, a lot of stuff comes from my grandparents' house and the objects I associate with their lives. Cold larders with chicken-mesh windows and ice cream cornets. I was able to dip into their world and remember all those things.

So you're filling it in from something within you. Is that why Bruegel's *The Fall of Icarus* is in the story?

I suspect that that picture is always there in my mind. And the Auden poem about it as well. *Musée des Beaux Arts*? The horse idly scratching its behind on a tree – all the things that are going on as Icarus is falling out of the sky.

Yes, he's just a little plop in the water. If it wasn't for the title, you wouldn't have known the picture was about that moment.

But in a way that picture is another version of those anchoring details in the story. It's significant, but it's also just a bright, memorable thing, highlighted and framed.

I felt that, if this story was about something, it was about kindness. I wondered if it was something of a counterpoint to the sinister element of threat and increasing horror in the story. Did you feel there were themes in the story?

Themes are the reader's job. It would be dangerous for me to think of themes or ideas, or attempt to persuade the reader of this or that.

I have this image in my mind of the writer being like the puppeteer in a Punch and Judy show. You're sat on a stool in the dark inside the tent, making all the voices, pulling the strings, moving the sticks up and down. You operate the secret internal mechanism according to the secret internal logic. But the only thing that matters in the end is what the audience sees at the front – you've got to make that experience as good as possible.

Occasionally, when I'm teaching writing, I tell writers: Don't try to get anything across. Just create a really good scene, make it work, entertain the audience. If you have a world view or a set of beliefs they will permeate the drama anyway. If you push any harder than that the reader usually pushes back. There's no need to push. The story will inevitably be flavoured with your view of the world.

A lot of people come to writing with the feeling they want to get something out of their heart or mind onto paper. I think, if you want to write seriously for other people you have to progress to a point where what's in your heart or your head is absolutely irrelevant – the relationship that matters is between the words on the page and the reader. The reader doesn't give a damn about what's going on in your head or heart, they only care about what's going on on the page. Some people find it hard to let go of that first stage because for them it's a kind of therapy, a kind of offloading. To them I'd say – it's an even better kind of therapy to let go of the ego and tell yourself, 'I will devote myself to making the story work and then release it out into the world'.

You are also a visual artist – are there any parallels between how you create in the different disciplines?

Yes and no. No, because what I love about making sculpture or painting is that I don't have to use any words whatsoever. Which is a relief when your head is full of language. Recently, because of long COVID, I've been finding writing very very hard, so being able to do something which is just about pictures in my head is a good deal easier.

But at the root of both visual art and literature is the rapid change of roles between creator and observer. Ultimately the question I always repeat is, 'Does this work?' You write or draw or paint something and then step back: 'Does it work?' It's a repeated asking of that question.

What do you mean by 'work'?

Does it move you? Does it give you some kind of frisson? Does it create something like the reaction you had to the art which made you want to become a writer or artist in the first place? Does it close that circle?

One of the difficulties of that is putting yourself in the mind of many different strangers. There's a weird disjunction between the extreme solitude of writing and the fact that you're trying to communicate with thousands and thousands of strangers – some of whom haven't been born yet. This huge community across time and space, across language, across culture. And you're just sitting at your desk at home, in your burrow. But sometimes, amazingly, it works.

Which is another set of extreme opposites…

Yes, it's a very strange thing to be creative. I find it hard to imagine being an artist working in a studio where assistants do your bidding, or being a playwright working on the hoof with actors sitting there waiting for a tweaked line, or being a TV writer who's part of a group in the white heat of the writing room. For me, the creative act demands the quiet and stillness of my own head. Only when I pause and describe it, do I realise what a profoundly odd activity it really is.

In *Duets*, I commissioned writers to write a story back and forth in pairs. If I had asked you to contribute, I imagine you wouldn't have been up for it?

I toyed for quite a long while with the idea of writing a graphic novel like that. Doing a page then handing it on to someone else for them to do a page and so on. It might have worked, but the lack of a guiding principle would have been a problem.

If a gun was held to my head and I had to work with someone else, we would have to work out the protocol. Do you do a chapter each and hand it back? A page? A paragraph? What I couldn't share with someone was the actual moment of creation, the shuffling of stuff around in my head. I need mental privacy to do that.

If so much is done in the editing, what is the writing like?

The two are often folded in together. When I come to write each day, I'll start three or four pages back from where I finished and edit back through to the end, and then add more on. It's like combing a particularly grubby long-haired dog – getting all the dirt and knots and burrs out until the comb runs smoothly.

Sometimes the editing is about structure. I'll notice that something is not working and I'll realise that I took a wrong turning a way back and have to retrace my steps. But usually the structure is sorted out early on and the editing is mostly about getting the surface smooth.

What does a 'smooth surface' look like?

Really pleasurable prose for me is where the next word feels both right and unexpected. And if you can do that then that's 90% of the battle won. If you keep going thinking, 'Oh yes, oh yes,' it will be fluid and organic and cohere really well. Even if it's thrillingly odd, it will feel unexpected but also correct.

Is there something you learnt about writing from writing 'The Bunker'?

The surprise for me is always how much I forget about writing. I finish a book or a story and I sit down to write something new and realise I don't have a clue. Which is better, I guess, than thinking, 'I know exactly how to do this.' Nevertheless, it's really shocking how soon it all seems to fall away. And how regularly I seem to be relearning basic principles that I've been sharing with students over the decades.

But does that make the story all the fresher, that it's not borne of a rule you keep to?

Hopefully, yes. Embrace your own naivety and idiocy and you might end up somewhere different.

Agata's Machine
by Camilla Grudova

Agata and I were both eleven years old when she first introduced me to her machine. We were in all the same classes. She was sallow and thin, with enormous hands and feet. She wore her dark brown hair in a short bob, held back from her face with a plain, plastic barrette. Her eyebrows weren't thick, but they were long, stretching to her temples. Her mouth was wide, but her lips were thin, with an expressiveness that reminded me of worms.

She wasn't tormented by our schoolmates and teachers, as I was. The only student they treated worse than me was Large Barbara, who was so fat she walked with a cane, had one lazy eyeball and a wart on her chin so long and thin it mocked the rest of her body. Agata wasn't teased or tormented because she was a genius. She excelled in the sciences and maths, and could write beautiful, complex poems, though she only did so when it was a school assignment. She often yawned and shook one of her legs in class; she finished her work before everyone else. Some teachers let her read her own books, imported ones in foreign languages, full of complicated diagrams just as mysterious to the rest of us as the words.

Though she wasn't bullied, she also didn't have any friends. She seemed above such trivialities. No one invited her to parties – it was impossible to imagine her at them. She spent her lunch break reading. She didn't play or gossip. She saw the other students as a nuisance, like flies or fleas. Some tried to pay her to do their homework, but she responded with, 'You think I don't have better things to do?' in a tone of voice that was arrogant, and delighted in its own arrogance, her worm mouth wiggling.

Agata's parents were poor because they had so many children, but they still bought her whatever she needed or desired so she could focus on her schoolwork: books, expensive pens, cigarettes. Agata was the eldest and the most promising of her siblings. The rest were snively, slow readers who wore second-hand clothes that had seen too many threadbare childhoods. Because their clothes were so old, so outdated, their hair so sparse, their limbs so rickety, and their foreheads so large, they looked like little old men, even the girls. Agata didn't care about clothes. I was sure her parents would buy her nice outfits, if she asked.

She wore cheap-looking floral dresses, meant for an older housewife, and large men's shoes – hand-me-downs from her father. When it was wet outside, she wore black rubber galoshes over her shoes, making her feet look even larger. In class she wore slippers of fuzzy grey wool.

I was vain and wore the same thin, white, feminine shoes all year round, even though the soles suffered under the pressure of my weight, and the material let water soak through, my toes and heels stained from the dye in my stockings. In class, I discreetly took my shoes off under my desk to let my feet dry, blue and black imprints on the inner lining of my shoes. These stains horrified and embarrassed me, as if the dye had come out of my body instead of my stockings.

One morning it was so wet outside that dyed water dripped from my feet onto the classroom floor. Agata, who was sitting behind me, whispered, 'Your foot is crying.'

She didn't say it loud enough for anyone else to hear, but I blushed.

Swiftly, she moved her own foot under my desk, and within a second the small puddle was gone.

She did it again and again, whenever a puddle formed, until my stockings, dry enough near the end of the day, ceased to drip.

Leaving class after school, she put her large hand on my arm and whispered in my ear. 'Come home with me, there's something I want to show you.'

I was filled with dread, as if a few more hours of class had been added to my day. What was she going to show me? Maths textbooks, a home laboratory kit? I was too afraid to say no, in case she would tell the rest of our class about my 'crying foot,' in case she would yell, loud enough for everyone to hear, 'Your foot cries!'

I was unsure whether I was embarrassed walking home with her or not. I didn't like the disgusting sound of her galoshes, the smell of her cigarettes, but she walked with such ease and confidence, with such disdain for everyone we passed by in our village. She wore fingerless gloves, a canvas knapsack so full it sagged down her legs, and a ragged blue military coat with flaking gold buttons.

Agata's family lived on the main floor of a five-floor building. The landlord allowed Agata to use the attic as a study. In exchange, Agata's father cleaned and maintained the foyer and the halls of the building, though he already had a full-time job as a clerk at a small glassware factory that specialised in vases.

Her mother, with all her other children, was too busy to clean the halls herself, said Agata. We briefly stopped in the family apartment before heading to her attic. There were children everywhere, and no sign of the life Agata lived; no books, only tacky lithographic prints of historic buildings, dark Madonna and Child icons dotting the walls like speckles on a crow's egg. I wondered if Agata had to share a bedroom with her siblings.

Her mother was thin and going bald. Her pregnant stomach was ridiculous and reminded me of a hard-boiled egg, a food no one at school would eat without shame because of its terrible smell and uncanny, wobbly movements once the shell was removed. She wore a cheap metal necklace, childish rings, and a dress just like Agata's. When introduced to her, I suppressed a giggle.

Agata didn't greet any of her younger siblings, but grabbed two bread rolls off the table.

'Bring us coffee in a bit,' she said to her mother, and pulled me out and upwards to her attic.

She unlocked the door with a key kept in one of her coat pockets, and took off her galoshes and shoes. She put on a pair of crusty-looking slippers from a ragged mat in the hall.

I also took off my shoes, but the floor of her attic was dirty, covered with peeling linoleum, carpet and patches of wood, a repulsive mixture that reminded me of bandages that needed to be changed and the flaky, scabby skin underneath.

The walls of Agata's attic were half-covered in maps and diagrams, a large poster of the periodic table, a map of the world. There were books everywhere, telescopes, glass vials, and microscopes. A green metal desk with a ragged, greasy armchair in front of it. A glass vase full of brown water and cigarette butts. Socks, papers, teacups and mousetraps – one with a flattened and dried mouse under its metal bar. I had assumed she would be meticulous and clean.

In the middle of the attic was something large and awkwardly shaped covered with a wool blanket. In one corner there was a headless garment dummy, its canvas torso covered in writing, too smudged to read. Agata took off her coat and hung it on the dummy. She lit a cigarette, and started to eat one of the rolls. She threw the other one to me. It was rock hard. I nibbled at it, but was used to finer things: my parents were grocers and I took pleasure in eating. For Agata, eating seemed like a distracting chore. She ate the bread roll with such indifference it could have been a raw potato or a marrow bone, she wouldn't have noticed.

After she finished it, and her cigarette, she rubbed her large, bony hands together and tore the blanket off the object in the centre of the attic. A gigantic black insect. It was a sewing machine, an old malicious one, black and gold, attached to its own desk with a treadle underneath, wrought metal like the grates over fire stoves and sewers. I was dumbfounded. Was she going to show me something both intricate and hideous that she had made? I knew from home economics class that she was a good sewer. If we finished a project before class was over, our teacher would make us mend her husband's socks, shirts, trousers, and underwear. Agata was the only one who didn't mind doing it; she was so indifferent to whatever cloth she was feeding the machine, and it was against her nature to sew deliberately slowly like the rest of us. So she pumped out, with spiritless speed, flat doppelgängers of the teacher's husband, the yellow pads of her tobacco-stained fingertips waltzing across the often unclean fabric which smelled like meat, soup, fruity liquors, and that fried-onions-and-mushroom scent which oozes from the bodies of grown men, as if they were nothing but sacks of unwanted leftovers. Our home economics teacher was sour-looking and had a moustache. Some of us believed her husband was imaginary, that she'd bring the newly sewn pieces home, fill them with slops and potatoes so they'd gain life-like proportions, and lie in bed with her creation, kissing it until the seams ripped, then bringing the pieces, ripped and stained with exaggeration, back to school with domestic pride, as if her husband was too large, too important, too filthy, too manly for her alone to manage.

At the sight of Agata's sewing machine, my imagination whirred.

Agata would make me a pair of stockings I wouldn't be able to take off. A pair that would swallow my legs and expand three-dimensionally with their own horrible breath, like balloons, that followed the direction of her will. She would cut me and sew me back up again like the baby toads she dissected with cold expertise in science class.

'My mother's old sewing machine, but that's not all,' she said.

I looked closer.

There was a large mason jar where the spool was supposed to go, perched on top of the sewing machine like a translucent egg being expelled from its body. Inside the jar was a cylindrical light bulb, the sepia colour of old photographs. Emerging from the top was a brown wire, attached like a thread to the levers and regulators before vanishing into a short wooden box where the needle was supposed to be. The wire reappeared from a small hole on the side of the box, ending in a black earpiece, culled from a telephone. The box had faded writing on the side. CIGARS, it said.

Agata pushed over her armchair and sat in front of the sewing machine. She started to pump the treadle. The large balance wheel started to turn, like a cinema reel. The jar started to move.

'Turn off the lights,' she said. I did, finding the switch near the door. The mason jar glowed. A wobbly bubble of light travelled across the room, then again, but this time there was some sort of shape inside it that was not fully formed, parts of it blacker than shadow, that morphed, flickering, into a Pierrot. He danced across the room. His face, white with black lips and eyebrows, was so beautiful I blushed. I blushed for him to see us, in Agata's filthy attic, our breath and armpits smelly from a day at school. His outfit was billowing white, with large black buttons, his feet small and pointed. I leaned against Agata's chair, watching the Pierrot circle us, again and again.

I knew what a Pierrot was. In my parents' shop, there was a porcelain Pierrot bust. He had rosy cheeks and the word *pierrot* was written across his chest. His shoulders were covered in holes to put lollipops in. The lollipops did not sell very well; children were afraid of the strange, foreign man with his black skullcap. My father had brought the Pierrot at an antique shop and thought it lent an air of elegance to his business. We had no idea what the original lollipops were like, and imagined horrible and exotic flavours – crab, liquorice, goat, octopus – rising from the Pierrot's shoulders, the sugar spun into monstrous shapes.

Agata didn't know the word 'Pierrot'; I taught it to her, and she was visibly grateful. It suited the handsome, romantic figure in her attic much better than 'clown'.

Agata handed me the earpiece. I didn't hear anything. It was more like being listened to, as if there was a piece of shivering flesh behind the plastic. I didn't see the Pierrot again, but this time appeared a man with white wings, wearing a striped sailor's shirt, and wide sailor's trousers. His hair was golden, greased back from his face, and his lips were red, very red, like he was wearing lipstick.

'I have never seen him before. I have only seen the Pierrot. This is why I wanted someone else to try it.' Agata put out her hand for the earpiece, pressed it to her ear, and the Pierrot appeared again. He performed a pirouette and blew us a kiss.

When she stopped treadling, I looked at the still jar. There were no images pasted onto it like on a lantern, or on the glass slides shown in class. I would have been disappointed if there had been: the winged man felt like something I had illustrated or brought into being.

Before Agata could start treadling again there was a knock on the door, a quiet, nervous tap. Without getting up from her chair, she gestured for me to open it and to turn on the light.

Her mother brought us cups of fake coffee made with chicory, and vanilla wafers that dissolved as soon as we put them in our mouths. Agata had a cigarette, then she told me to turn the light off again.

I didn't get home till late. My parents were pleased to hear I had been studying with Agata, for her intelligence was known around our whole village. The next morning I hoped, more than anything, that Agata would ask me to come over again. She did. I wasn't sure if she liked my company, or only wanted to see the 'angel' man again, but either way it didn't matter. I went every day, after school. Agata even borrowed a chair from her family's apartment for me to sit on. It was a toddler's chair, with short squat legs, the seat bedecked with colourful illustrations of dogs and flowers. Agata never let me pump the treadle of her machine.

By the time I went home each night I was starving, and my dinner, left on the table with a cloth on top, was lukewarm.

I was used to having a snack as soon as I got home from school, and I got into the habit of stealing things from my family's shop for Agata and me to eat. I brought hazelnut wafers, caramel chews, soft iced-ginger cookies, dry sausages, bottles of raspberry syrup we mixed with water, preserved plums covered in chocolate and, at Agata's request, an expensive brand of cigarettes with a picture of Romeo and Juliet on the packet, imported from a country in the Caribbean.

My father noticed I was taking things, and though he was glad I was studying (it was easy to lie to him about that), he couldn't afford such indulgences, and from then on only allowed me to take food from the overstock room. It was full of large jars of plum jam, dark brown in colour, and tinned sardines. Besides the cigarettes, it didn't make much difference to Agata. We ate the plum jam straight from the jar using spoons. I hated sardines, but Agata ate them, peeling off the silver skin and spitting out the bones.

My parents and I lived above our shop. We didn't share any walls with neighbours, and I was fascinated by Agata's building. It reminded me of the cabinet with dozens of tiny drawers where my parents kept precious seeds and spices. I became obsessed by the fantasy that the angel and Pierrot lived somewhere in the building, that their images had travelled through pipes and oozed through the attic walls like leaking water. When I confessed it to Agata, she called me an idiot, but I couldn't concentrate on the machine until she'd introduced me to every neighbour. Every door was a disappointing drawer, full of tiny sticky flecks and withered cinnamon sticks. A breath of hope before the next one, then again, nothing. Finally, every room in the building had been emptied of my dreams, except the attic. I also begged her to let me see inside the cigar box. It was nothing to me; a tangle of wires and cogs, no tiny Pierrot and angel trapped inside like beautiful white mice in a cage.

The moving images came from us, or were connected to us, Agata couldn't say exactly. She had made the machine in order to project images from her mind's eye, but the Pierrot wasn't anything she had seen or imagined before. The angel was just as new to me.

I remembered once visiting my aunt in the city, when she took me to an arcade where a fortune teller lived in a theatrical box with glass sides. The fortune teller, who wore a colourful turban and many jewels, was made from wax, with a silent wax mouth. If you put a coin in a slot underneath the glass, she released a tiny card with your future written on it. Mine said I would get married and have one child. Agata's machine must have said something about our futures, for where else could the images come from?

I created beautiful and ridiculous scenarios in my mind. I was married to the angel, Agata to the Pierrot. The angel and I owned a small, white dog. I spent hours imagining how he would bathe without getting his wings wet, how I would stroke them and keep all the feathers that fell off in a red lacquered box.

I even dreamed that Agata's Pierrot was secretly in love with me, that he was in a sense enslaved by her. In fact, he felt somehow originally mine, because of the Pierrot bust in my parents' shop. I knew the word, and had given it to her.

I knew Agata had fantasies too, but hers were perhaps filled with more knowledge of the world. Just as she knew how to smoke cigarettes without coughing and read foreign languages, so could she construct an imaginary marriage much more thorough than mine.

Sometimes she would suddenly say, 'Leave now.' The light continued moving after I left – I could see it under the door where I would stand until my legs hurt. I know she wanted to view the images in private. I never complained, I was too afraid of being banned from her machine forever. There was something in the way she said it – 'Leave' – that made her seem more grown up than me. Yet we were dependent on each other like a pair of twins, conjoined by a dream rather than a body, for the angel appeared more often when I held the machine to my ear, and the Pierrot when she did. The machine, our secret, bound us together: I could tell her parents or our classmates, while she could tell my parents I wasn't studying.

We weren't friends, exactly. I was bothered by the sound of her breathing and sniffing, she always had a runny nose, and she often screamed at me for sucking my teeth or for noisily passing gas. Our bodies were nuisances to the enjoyment of the machine. I asked my father if I could borrow his record player, which folded up neatly into a suitcase. Music greatly enhanced the whole experience as it made it seem like our dear friends were not silent and unbreathing but, like us, merely drowned out by the music.

The colour of the attic's walls, the greyish pink wallpaper with its pattern of green ferns curled like little goblins' ears, gave the angel and Pierrot the appearance of having a skin disease. I didn't notice this detail in my initial enchantment, but it became noticeable as I demanded more from the machine, like a stomach expanding from eating an ever-increasing amount of food.

I had the idea of painting the walls white, but Agata didn't approve – it would mean days away from the machine, she didn't want paint to get on her books, she didn't want to pack up her things – so I constructed a white collage along her walls using a white linen tablecloth, a large white blouse of my mother's, some sheets of typing paper, cloth bags for sugar and flour from the grocery store, endpapers ripped out of books, a piece of wooden board I painted white myself and carried over. Any white scrap I could find. Agata agreed: the angel and Pierrot looked purer, fuller, against white.

I had a dream that I removed all my teeth and glued them to the walls. I removed Agata's teeth too, but they were stained and crooked, as in real life. As soon as I extracted them they started to grow until they were the size and length of elephant tusks. They smelled like soiled laundry and were covered in tiny black cavities.

Once, Large Barbara tried to follow us home, as if she could smell we were up to something important. We ran, Large Barbara's cane rattling against the stones of the streets behind us. It was a horrible cane, with a doll's head on the top, soiled and squished by Large Barbara's sweaty hand. She screamed and screamed, irregular sounds, like the varied contents of a small, travelling menagerie, her cane a large beak or claw hitting the bars. She couldn't catch up.

We didn't mention the incident once we were upstairs, but the attic contained a thought too repellent to voice: what would Large Barbara, who was hopeless, an idiot, see with her ear against the machine? If she were to see, for example, a beautiful prince, wearing turquoise trousers and a yellow sash, it would mean the machine had no base in the future, or reality, and was nothing more than a reflection of our desires.

I don't remember the date of the day Mr. Magnolia first appeared. All days had melted into each other, into an amber-coloured syrup that slowly hardened under the whirring of Agata's machine.

I do remember that Agata was holding the earpiece the first time Mr. Magnolia appeared.

He was bald, except for a thin rim of hair like scum on a dirty bowl and a plain, unfanciful moustache shaped like the little plastic combs used for lice searches at school. He was old, like a father, and wore a suit, a drab, ill-fitting grey one.

As he moved across the room he sneered, stuck his tongue out, and grabbed his crotch, his mouth open in a silent laugh.

We both gasped, but Agata didn't stop treadling her machine.

The next round, the Pierrot reappeared, as if nothing had changed; then my angel, then Pierrot and the strange old man again, in an odd, nonsensical sequence.

Agata kept pumping, horrified and transfixed.

'Mr. Magnolia,' she whispered, then added, 'The name came to me as he appeared. They must come from the same place, they must belong to each other.'

'I don't know, I heard that word somewhere, yes, it's his name.'

She looked the word up in her seven-volume dictionary. The different volumes were scattered around her attic and it took us a while to find L–M. We were surprised to learn that magnolia was a flower, a large pink or white one. The dictionary did not contain pictures or any more information, so we could only imagine how horrible the flower must be. We went to a flower shop.

'Do you have any magnolias?' I stumbled over the word, unsure if we were being obscene.

'Magnolias grow on trees, I can't sell a bushel of them. I have beautiful purple asters, poppies, carnations, roses. Silly girls, magnolias grow on trees!' said the shop owner, a broad woman with dyed hair and too much make-up, wearing a wet and stained apron over her dress.

Agata blushed at the word 'silly'. It was the first time I had ever seen her blush.

'Here, I'll show you a picture.' The shop owner went into the back of her shop, returning with a large, damp book.

'It can either be white, or pink. Girls, it grows on trees in foreign places!' she laughed. The flower looked like a dessert.

'Stupid, worthless dictionary. It should've told us that,' Agata mumbled as we left. We walked back to her house in a hurry, both wanting to see Mr. Magnolia again, to compare him with the image of the flower we had just seen. But there was no resemblance between the beautiful, large flower and the ugly plainness of Mr. Magnolia, who grimaced at us and tugged at his trouser legs.

'Mr. Magnolia, he must come from abroad. That is the connection. Perhaps he has an important message,' said Agata when we were back in her attic.

We recorded and tried to decode all his poses, gestures, and faces, but it was really a way to kill time between seeing the Pierrot or the angel who struck us dumb. Whatever music was playing when Mr. Magnolia appeared was made ridiculous. We could never play that song again. As Mr. Magnolia continued to appear, more and more songs were ruined. I borrowed more records from my father's collection – symphonies, ballets, operas, folk songs – and was careless with the ones we no longer wanted, tossing them across the attic. They cracked and were forgotten.

Sometimes Agata would say, 'I am so sick of Mr. Magnolia, thank you very much,' or 'Fuck you and your Mr. Magnolia,' her lips curled, her head turned in my direction.

It was unfair of her to blame me for Mr. Magnolia. He first appeared when the earpiece was held against her head. He slithered out of her mind like a maggot. Was he waiting to prance, like a devil, into both of our futures?

I lost weight, I smelled like tobacco. I was behind on my schoolwork. My teachers had written my parents a letter, so they knew. Agata wasn't. She didn't hand in assignments anymore either, but I think the teachers believed she could do no wrong; they were firm in the belief that her work would be the best in class if she handed it in, so it wasn't necessary for her to do so. She didn't speak in class anymore, but sat sullenly, her arms crossed, one foot underneath her desk moving up and down as if pressing an invisible treadle.

Neither of us had appetites, our stomachs felt tight and curled like unblossomed flowers. We consumed only cigarettes, cups of black tea, and spoonfuls of plum jam, brown and glistening like grease to smooth the cogs of a machine.

One evening, returning home bleary-eyed, my fingers sticky, my parents forbade me from returning to Agata's. My mother said it was disgusting for a family to have so many children, and that she had heard they all slept in one big bed, boys and girls mixed. My mother picked me up from school the next day, and the next, and also dropped me off in the morning. The first night away from Agata's machine, I couldn't sleep.

'What happened?' I asked Agata as soon as we were seated in class.

'Nothing. The same. Mr. Magnolia appeared fifty times, Pierrot twenty times.'

'And my angel?'

'Not once. He only appears when you are in the room.'

The thought gave me relief and hope. Had the angel missed me? Did he not think it worth appearing if I wasn't there?

Still, I worried he would appear for Agata alone the next day. Every morning I asked her, and she gave the same reply. After four days, she answered, 'Yes. He blew me a kiss.'

'No. I'm joking,' she snorted, when my face gave away my horror.

After a week, I stopped asking her, though she still told me. I acted indifferent, and it started to make me feel indifferent.

I felt calmer, more focused. I could read, do my homework. My appetite returned, my parents indulging whatever edible whims I had.

The time came, a few weeks later, when I felt assured that I could see Agata's machine again without the intensity of feeling I had before.

I was even glad at the thought of seeing Mr. Magnolia, but mostly I was curious to see how my reappearance would affect the expressions of the angel and Pierrot. Of course, my parents wouldn't let me, so I had to sneak out after dark. I was sure Agata would be running her machine throughout the night, and I was right. The angel and Pierrot didn't act any differently than before; I was disappointed, I had expected them to jump off the wall and embrace me. All I could do was continue holding the earpiece to my scalp, for Agata to continue pumping. There was a jar of plum jam left over from my last visit, viscid because the cap hadn't been put back on properly. We ate it from the jar with our fingers, the earpiece increasingly sticky as we passed it between us.

'Faster! Move it faster!' I screamed, Mr. Magnolia disappearing as quickly as he appeared, his image not fully formed, his head oddly squished and wobbly.

I barely focused on my angel when he appeared, so keen to see him a second time. 'C'mon, again!' I screamed as he was pulled back into the lantern. I kicked away my little chair, sat on Agata's lap and put my foot over hers, adding pressure. My foot was much smaller, it didn't make her go any faster, but she put her free arm around my waist and held me there, and the earpiece passed seamlessly between us. The angel and Pierrot became stronger, more flamboyant in their actions. The angel imitated the obscene crotch-grabbing of

Mr. Magnolia, and I was so thrilled that at first I did not hear my father shouting in the hall. I did not hear him until he had grabbed me, and was carrying me away, and only then I noticed that my legs and arms and nightdress were covered in jam, so dark it could have been blood. Perhaps my father imagined it was.

At home, my mother bathed me, calling me disgusting over and over again, while I moaned, a strange, deep sound I had never made before. I did not go to school the next day; I did not go to that school ever again. I suffered from horrible visions: Agata's lips, Mr. Magnolia's crotch, jars of jam with bits and pieces of sewing machines hidden inside that I choked on, they tasted like metal and liquorice. I kicked and screamed and threw up, and was kept in my room for months.

When I could get out of bed, I was sent to stay with my aunt in the city. My parents sold the shop and joined me a few months later. By then I was so integrated into my aunt's exciting city life that our village, and my entire childhood, was a blur I was embarrassed to remember. My aunt took me to restaurants, bookshops, department stores, markets, and the cinema. She was a professor, and though she lived alone, she had many male friends. I became fond of one, Leopold. He was much older than me. He had a raspberry-coloured birthmark on his cheek and wore very tiny, round spectacles. I kept in touch with him throughout my schooling, and married him when I started university. Our son inherited his father's gigantic nose, which depressed Leopold sometimes, as his nose was full of cruel, bitter memories like an old heart, but I liked it. They both made me think of crows with their feathers painted pink.

I found work as an archivist and often looked for Agata's name in catalogues and newspapers, but I found no trace of her. I assumed she'd gone abroad, perhaps taken on a different name to fit in better. It was hard to return to our country, and I felt bad for her parents, who had put so much effort into supporting her, most likely getting nothing in return.

I still suffered, a little. I couldn't stand any sort of apparatus. Leopold once gave me a music box shaped like a theatre with a dancing paper Pierrot inside. It made me so nervous I had to run to the bathroom and vomit. I couldn't even hang a mobile above our son's crib because of the shadows it would project across his nursery walls.

I hated the microfilm readers at work, I avoided them as much as possible, and typewriters, which I used sparingly, always biting my tongue. I preferred to make handwritten labels and lists, and made sure my handwriting was neat and clear so my co-workers wouldn't complain.

My favourite things to work with were old manuscripts, so old I had to wear white gloves while handling them, manuscripts written on skin. I couldn't think about the way clothes were made, with those awful, black contraptions. I was drawn to expensive things described as 'hand woven', 'hand knitted'; I loved the word 'hand', its warm and soft connotations. I always imagined a chubby, pink child's hand like my son's, completely opaque – no wiry veins showing underneath.

I hated anything that whirled, flickered, buzzed, clicked, clattered. Sometimes I had nightmares, beasts with scissor mouths, metal fan wings, a telephone receiver for eyes, metal pincers and cog wheels longing to touch me.

There aren't any flattering photos of me. Cameras make me blink and shudder.

I still took great pleasure in food, with the exception of fish and jam. Fish did not seem natural, but mechanical somehow, perhaps because of their silver skins. I often had a dream in which Agata scooped out my flesh with a long spoon and stuffed it into fish skins made from silver satin and sewed the seams onto her machine. I was left as nothing but a pile of fake sardines, the satin damp from my flesh hidden inside, and a skeleton wearing my own hair as a wig.

For my birthday, Leopold always gave me cured ham legs, pickled tongues, and other gourmet meats, ones that resembled what they were, meat that hadn't been minced, ground, pulverised.

When I was in my forties, I went back to our old village to visit a sick aunt who was too weak to travel to the city. I had the idea that I would also visit Agata's mother, remembering the cruel way I used to laugh at her bald patches, her skinny limbs. I also suspected my parents had given her harsh words. I wanted to show her that she was forgiven, that really it wasn't her fault. I would bring her flowers.

I looked for the old flower shop, but it was gone. There was a floral section in a large, new grocery store. I bought her a cheery orange bouquet.

The curtains in the first floor windows of their building were faded from the sun, and full of equally faded trinkets, like deteriorating daguerreotypes that took the interior life of the building with them as they crinkled and vanished, leaving nothing but a blank stone wall, an uninhabited ruin.

I was surprised to find anyone there. Agata's mother answered their door.

She wore a turban made of ragged grey and black fabric, from which I surmised that she must be entirely bald underneath. She was even thinner than I remembered, and bent, like a rib bone. The apartment was free of children; they were all grown up by now. Instead there was an old man, huddled in a chair by the stove, giving off the same sopping smell as a toddler. I wondered how many of their children had left the town, how many had left our country, to which they could never return.

'Come upstairs,' her mother said in a whisper, placing the flowers on the table. Agata's father flared his nostrils, seeking the origin of the floral smell, and I realised that he was blind.

'From the glass. His eyes were ruined by the glass,' Agata's mother said, shuffling out. I followed her up the stairs. There was a distinctive mixture of aromas – cabbages, shoe polish, mice, tobacco, old kitchen pipes, walnuts, smoked ham – as if the stairwell was an accordion, and each step a key that released not a note, but a heavy spray of fragrance. It was the thought of being trapped in that wheezing, terrible contraption that made me hesitate, but Agata's poor mother kept walking up, and so I followed. Strongest was a warm, waxy smell. It drowned out all the others in great, deep waves, and I had the sensation I was ascending towards a room full of thousands of burning tallow candles.

By the time I glimpsed the buttery light under the door, I knew what to expect, and my ears took in the flickering sound.

She sat in the same armchair. She was so fat that her eyes, which used to protrude, were sunk deep into the flesh of her face, as if they were drowning in the bluish purple bags below them. She was lumpy and frayed, like a cloth doll stuffed with too much wool. Unclean fleece, I thought, torn from an animal. Her brown hair was cut short, and was oily. I could see layers of dandruff flakes stuck to her hairline, glistening in the light of her lantern, like shards of broken glass among the wooden ruins of a building. In the centre was a bald spot; an unclean skylight, cracked like a boiled egg tapped with a spoon, but still solid.

'The angel hasn't come back since you left. He is waiting for you,' she said, only half-looking at me and her mother, who whispered, 'I'll bring you girls some coffee in a few hours,' and left.

My white collage on the wall had turned yellow. Scraps of fresh paper, mostly toilet roll, ribbons, and a fridge door had been added. It resembled a frilled and bedraggled wedding dress, ill-preserved by its bride, worn over and over again, the sweat and sweetness of the wedding day covered in grey reproductions of itself, the stains of a day relived over and over. I imagined the attic as one of the arched hollows under the bride's arm, the place where the body leaves its imprint on fabric most intensely, those pathetic, damp, and silent mouths of the heart.

My old chair was very small, it hurt my back, the earpiece was greasy, but I felt behind it that strange piece of flesh, that mysterious ear listening to me. Once more my winged man appeared, wearing the same appealing wide-wool trousers, the same lipstick, and I thought, he's feigning cheery indifference, he is yellowed and worn by my absence.

Keep the Path Submerged:
Camilla Grudova on 'Agata's Machine'

Camilla Grudova lives in Edinburgh. She holds a degree in Art History and German from McGill University, Montreal. Her fiction has appeared in *The White Review* and *Granta*.

Camilla and I spoke about her use of the senses to form her stories; her use of images, colours and even smells.

What was the first inkling that started you writing 'Agata's Machine'?

I think it came from what I was consuming culturally at the time. I had just finished my university degree in German literature and film where we studied Lotte Reiniger – an animator in the 1920s. She made silhouette films, cutting everything out and then putting it onto a projector. I found the craftiness of her process really fascinating.

The Pierrot came from my mom. She really loves Pierrots – they're special to Eastern European culture, people there really relate to that clown the way they relate to Eeyore from Winnie the Pooh. He's a very melancholic figure.

I was also drawn to the Pierrot in the film *Children of Paradise*, and listened to a lot of songs by Alexander Vertinsky. He was an inverted Pierrot – he wore a black outfit with white buttons instead of a white outfit with black buttons.

He had a song with the word 'Magnolia' in it, a famous old Russian song. So, I was listening to that, and I think those things combined with memories and stuff.

Did you have a sense of what you were going to do with these ingredients? Maybe how you were going to blend them? Or did you just get going?

I just got going. Certain things just stick to each other in your brain and make a pattern. And it starts with that, rather than it being something conscious that I'm setting out – the things feel like they belong together, like I'm putting together a puzzle that will make an intriguing image.

Did you come up with the idea of the narrator and her childhood friend knowing that you would get to the Pierrot and Mr. Magnolia later?

I think the Pierrot appeared first and then I gave him an audience. I was in my early twenties when I wrote the story and fascinated by girlhood and looking back at my own. So that kind of first-person narration of a young, young woman felt quite natural as well.

Was there something about girlhood and coming of age you wanted to explore?

I don't think I consciously went in with that intention. I don't think I ever go in *consciously*. I start to write something, have a feeling for it, and then afterwards realise what I wanted to explore – that works better, to keep the path submerged in the unconscious as you're writing; things might become too obvious to the writer if they're conscious of them.

But it definitely is about childhood. When my cousin read it, she said, 'This reminds me of when we were 11 or 12 and would go on Harry Potter chat rooms and talk to strangers who were probably creepy old men pretending to be children.' I think it must have been quite influenced by that time.

Although it also comes from my phobia of video games. I find them quite claustrophobic, and I think my repulsion or fear fed the story.

The repulsion of the machine?

Yeah, the video game world. I sound very Victorian but it doesn't do anything for you; there is something very static about just entering a video game, not even knowing how much time has passed when you emerge from it. It doesn't help you navigate the world in a way that literature can.

So Agata's machine is a bit like a video game for you?

Yeah, I've seen the dangers of becoming completely immersed.

Although it's also about daydreams. I'm a big daydreamer and a lot of my stories start that way. But I think it can be kind of life-sucking and dangerous as well – especially when I feel like my life never matches up to how I want it to be, which means you just get sucked into daydreams, which is probably counter-productive and makes your life even less how you want it to be.

I wondered if Agata's machine was like an early cinema, with its projector and home-made screen – but is it not as simple as that?

That's interesting. Recently – after I wrote the story – I visited the Lumiere brothers' house in France, which is now a museum. They used sewing machines and guns as prototypes to figure out how to make moving images. Maybe I read about these things and forgot about them. It must have stuck in my brain somehow. I find that era of cinema really fascinating.

There's a lot of description of Agata's appearance and all of her belongings and what she wore. Did you have a sense of her and then worked towards what her things would be like, or did you discover more about Agata from her things?

Maybe somewhere in between, but I do think physical things really help me build up characters. Some people might view that as shallow, but I really struggle with abstract thoughts. I have a very visual mind so if I think of an abstract concept I'll need a physicality and an image in order to think about an idea.

You have said that you really like lists. Do they do something similar? Form something like the physical manifestations of ideas?

Yeah, I could read just a book of lists and really enjoy it. I can look at a word – if it's a nice-looking word – and then look through it, like a little window, at the thing as well.

George Perec's *Life: A User's Manual* was a big influence on my list-making. And also Horace Walpole, who wrote *The Castle of Otranto*, had a book he kept republishing that was a list of everything in his house at Strawberry Hill. I feel it's the first piece of modernist British literature. Every time he bought one more thing he had to publish a new edition of his book. It's written in that beautiful old Eighteenth-Century English as well so it's really lovely to read, as well as seeing all his things.

So you have an infinite tolerance for a list?

Yes, I would love a whole novel that was like just a list – maybe someday I'll do that.

When we read about the machine, the story becomes frictionlessly unreal and magical. And yet at other times the narrator is very meticulous, setting out details which might feel a bit superfluous considering we've suspended our disbelief already. What do these little details add to such a surreal story?

I think you need to be able to describe things and furniture in a plain style. I think you need those things or the story will fly away into incomprehensibility, some sort of 1960s acid-like vision, which is an aesthetic I hate.

I think it's something I got from the Surrealists. Their paintings have a really strong sense of perspective: the idea that you need to be a good draftsman before you can distort reality. There's a really beautiful scene in *Life is Elsewhere* by Milan Kundera: a painter is showing a student Salvador Dali paintings because the student was trying to do surreal things without being able to draw things in a regular way. I apply that to literature – though I don't agree you have to write strictly realistically before you can write something really weird.

I love how your story ranges here and there. There's parts that a cloth-eared editor might question for not corresponding clearly to other parts. What do you feel about the idea that a story is better for its unity?

I feel that the vision some people have of short stories is quite conservative. Which is weird because they are like, 'Oh, short stories don't sell, they're not important,' but at the same time are quite stringent about what it should look like in a way that they aren't with novels or poetry.

I feel the shape of my story quite intuitively – I can visualise it as really gooey or doughy, something that I'm forming. Everything that's in the story makes sense in my own logic: all these components belong together.

Do you feel like you're breaking rules?

In A.S. Byatt's introduction to *The Oxford Book of English Short Stories*, she says all the stories in the collection break the rules about what is expected of them. I really agree with this – I feel that if it works, it works, and if you can find a new way to break the rules then it's quite exciting.

As opposed to a novel, the short story is a bit like a blue cheese that would be hard to consume in large quantities – which means there's more possibilities for the surreal because you're not there for as long.

These parts that maybe didn't tie together explicitly had instead quite intriguing distances between them. Are these intentionally fable-like?

Absolutely, yes, I think I am quite influenced by fairy tales. I see them as the original short stories. People like to separate them and say, 'Oh no, the short story was a nineteenth-century magazine invention,' but I would say fairy tales were short stories – perhaps they've been seen as less significant because they were often created by marginalised groups, like working class women, or like Aesop, who was a slave.

It feels that in this very conservative view of what a short story is, people try to fix an upper-middle class respectability to it and sever its ties to these older forms.

What is it about the fable that you like to use in your work?

I like the dead-pan style. There's never a character gasping in disbelief. I don't think I have time for all those novels where someone asks, 'What is this? I don't know what's going on!' You don't need to do that – as long as you have confidence then the reader is going to believe you.

Angela Carter took up the theme of the fairy tale but writers like Leonora Carrington and Barbara Comyns took up the style. I think that nowadays, people are taught a plainer style of language, and so don't see it as revolutionary as they used to.

And is there something more universal and essential about harking back to the fairy tale?

Yeah, with its plainer language it's less obscuring. As a visual reader, you want the story to be small elaborate windows that you look through at something, rather than having to slog through a bunch of abstract Latin words in order to make a vision in your head.

You've said how the apparitions – Mr. Magnolia, the Pierrot, the winged sailor – first came to you. I know you didn't want to think too consciously about them as you wrote but when you read the story again, did you get a glimpse of any significance they have in the story?

The angel sailor guy I always saw as a Fauvist painting – a very colourful pre-World War Two image that is very pleasing to me. Mr. Magnolia is probably just an image that's repulsive and funny: that he's named after a beautiful flower although a crotch-grabbing moustachioed dirty old man.

Making these fantastical male figures was funny, because they were jarring perhaps.

I think my own brain works in the same invasive way. You can sit down to a nice daydream and then something hideous just comes out and enters against your own will.

So once you've introduced these appealing images, how do you want them to affect the story?

It is mainly about making a specific picture to put into the reader's head. With this, I thought, 'How can these visions affect the other images and have an effect on what we have seen of the girls.'

I have a very strong emotional reaction to the story – I feel from the images something very resonant and moving takes shape. At what point does the story reach this stage for you?

Not until it's finished, I think. And even now, it has resonances that it didn't for me at the time. I was still probably more hopeful when I was younger; I don't think I would be able to write that story now because it would be too close to home. I had a weird experience recently when I realised I don't daydream about the future anymore, I just daydream about the past – which was very depressing to realise that I'm only ever now trying to rewrite the past.

When I read it recently I was interested in the element of female fantasy in it. I wrote this over ten years ago, and I feel that female fantasy has grown to become more prominent in the literary world, for example with the rise of Romantasy, and Sally Rooney's books, which seem to portray men as fantasy projections.

I was also interested in the portrayal of technology in it. I was thinking about the old chat forums with the green background and pink font. I'm hesitant to write directly about contemporary technology so I like to use older things as an analogy. I think I was trying to do that: using the analogy of early film to try and process what's happening in our lives at the time. I liked using things that have become almost archetypal or lived beyond their uses, like old sewing machines.

So, like the fairy type, going back to the archetype to make the work universal?

Yeah, exactly.

Mr. Magnolia appears after a break, in a new section which feels slightly different in texture to the earlier section – I wondered if you had written this new section in a different day's writing. How separate was this new section for you?

That I can't remember. I know some of the stories in that collection I just wrote in a day. I wrote it a lot faster than I write now; I didn't have a smartphone so I had all this good concentration.

The break must have been the narrator having some disillusionment with Agata, mixed in with her repulsion of Mr. Magnolia, as though he is part of her friend: 'This man comes from your brain, you're the repulsive one.'

Yes, I was really intrigued by their relationship. As they grow up, their relationship shifts and fluctuates, they become both more intimate and then increasingly suspicious of each other. It wondered if there was something particular in how you wrote them?

139

I guess it was inspired by friendships and also sibling relationships. There's something terrible about having shared childhood memories with another kid. It feels almost too intimate, especially when you're growing up – you want to get away from those deep intimacies. There's such a meanness as well, like when they are cruel to Large Barbara. Primary School children can terrify others with their nicknames – they really find their weaknesses and point them out.

Agata is described as 'indifferent' quite a few times so I was surprised that at the end she was waiting for the narrator? It felt like there was a dependency that wasn't clear until the last moment.

When I think of past relationships or past memories, stepping back into them can feel quite claustrophobic and repulsive. I wanted that final scene to have that feeling.

It also had to do with going home for a bit after university and seeing that family situations were a lot worse than I imagined, seeing things now as a grown-up and getting drawn back into it. Which I guess was a fear of mine: getting drawn back into family dynamics too much.

And the ending came as a surprise because Agata – who had been so independent and brilliant – as an adult didn't even seem to leave the room; nothing became of her, which was sad. I wondered how much the story was about disappointment and frustration, especially after the fanciful and magical projections of the screen, when – fairytale-like – the narrator is put in her room for three months and everything accelerates away from

her. After such a strong sense of their 'becoming', they never get to 'be' the adult person. Or if the narrator does, she is only described as a wife and a mother from thereon. Was that a storyline you intentionally decided on?

I think it was something unconscious. Reading it now I'm older and less hopeful, I see those bits more. As a kid, your fantasies feel that they might be a real possibility. But in the end the narrator and Agata give into the fantasy, there was no speck of reality or potentiality left in it. It was pure fantasy. I'm kind of like that with my daydreams now.

It feels maybe a bit prescient because it's a real slap round the face for optimism and daydream. Maybe you had that in you even then?

Yes, like a weird message to me from my past self.

'Coming of age' has become a bit of a cliché from Hollywood films but it *is* such an intensely emotional time, trying on who you want to be – I wondered if the narrator was so uncomfortable being herself that Agata initially represented a way to be something else?

Yes, I think when you're a kid, you have friends you admire and want to be like, until you feel like you have moved beyond them in some ways and not in others, so that when you're older the whole relationship and how you saw them becomes less intense. You don't idealise them anymore. I felt I was always one of those people who were drawn to charismatic figures.

Yes, the first flush of a friendship is almost romantic, feeling so excited by this new person.

Yeah, and there's always just some disillusionment or change, when you don't see a friend living up to their potential after they seemed like your most brilliant friend in school.

I felt that there was a cooling about two thirds into the story, when the narrator says: 'I acted indifferent and it started to make me indifferent.' Was this an intentional lowering of the story's stakes and intensity?

Maybe the whole opening bit seemed a bit claustrophobic and a bit smelly in its own way. Maybe the reader – and I – needed to step back a bit before diving back in. It may have needed that release or that contrast in some way, like a chiaroscuro.

So you are thinking about story as well as just the constellating of images?

Yeah, though it's hard, as I feel like I'm one of those people who struggle to say what a plot is. I always feel like I have plots but people say, 'This is a completely plotless book!' So, to me, it's a story that tunes itself around the images and just forms. I would never rewrite a story because it feels like it has its own destiny and even if it is not a very good story then that is what it is.

I guess there's lower stakes with a short story. Though I put a lot of thought into them, there's not that fussing over it that I do with novels.

I like the idea that a story has its own destiny. What quality would a story have for you to feel it's found its destiny?

I think of it like a piano that is tuned so it can play the thing, even though it only has one specific thing to play. When you have an idea, it is like having a certain amount of dough, which you can't stretch too far or make too dense, or else it will be formless.

I think it will also have a genuineness to it in order for it to work. I feel a story that has been grappled with and rewritten many times won't work because that aspect can get lost in it.

I will feel quite satisfied if I cannot see the whole thing in my brain but 'nearly see it' as a form, so I'll know, 'Okay, that's it'. There also has to be something in it that has to make me laugh a bit – it won't feel fully successful if it's too serious.

So freshness is important?

Yeah, I feel sometimes when you have a story that has been worked over it almost a B.O. smell to it. Especially with the short story, there has to be something really unconscious and really fresh.

You've mentioned smells a few times as a criterion you judge a story against. Is that something you feel almost explicitly when you're thinking about your work?

Yeah, I want it to have lots of flavour. I wonder if that gives a strong form to it. I don't like stories that are really wispy and abstract and don't leave you with the *sense* of it. I really try and have all the senses engaged in the story.

Which might be the reason that, even though this story is magical, this story leaves me with a greater sense of the tactility of the wood and the 'thinginess' of the world.

Yes, the callus of it.

You have said that you like to start a story from a colour. Was this an influence on 'Agata's Machine'?

Definitely, throughout the whole book of *The Doll's Alphabet* I had a colour palette; those sepia colours, a black-and-white, a light pink colour, there's a lot of mossy-green colour in it. I may not use those words explicitly but those are the colours I wanted the book to keep near to.

I think it might be a bit of synaesthesia; I feel that different words have certain colours. When I go to concerts, I'll see a silvery spaghetti thing that is floating in the air in my brain. I think that has an effect on how I write.

Why does the story end on the image of the angel? When I read the ending, I did that thing that crap readers do and turned the page thinking the story would continue – your ending didn't have that timbre of a writer slowing to a stop. Instead, it kept its propulsion, which I find a really strong element in your writing, that sense of furtherance. For example, this ending is in the present tense, which makes it feel very current. Could you say what was important for you as you finished the story?

I guess I wanted the reader to feel that somewhere Agata and the narrator are still in that room, still looking at the images. I struggle with the very neatly tied-up ending – I think I do end a lot of stories suddenly, but that's just where it ends in my mind. I feel if you tie it up then it's no longer still existing, where I want it to be still going on somewhere in the world which you're stepping away from.

Was there anything in the writing of this story – or in the collection at about that time – that you learnt about writing?

It was the book where I really found my style when I was writing it. Obviously I want to move on and improve but that was the first time I felt I had tapped into something unique. I had a lot of half-finished novels in the drawer but I don't think I had conceived of writing a short story collection until I had the permission of signing a contract for writing a book. I thought, 'Okay, so this is a project I get to do.'

I had influences for the book – like Bruno Schulz, Kafka, Angela Carter, Barbara Comyns – who I was able to take things from and then find my own flavour. I was proud of myself for doing that. That basis is still something I work from and return to.

Was it the very literal license given from the publishing contract that allowed you to make this progression in your craft?

In terms of it being a book, yeah. There were a few stories we left out of the book that I don't think I'd put in another one – they feel very much of that time and the person I was then.

Mr Blythe Esq.

by Amber Medland

Typing I

Today my boss handed me an envelope, then a stamp, and told me to lick it.

My online therapist, Susan, says that my inability to set appropriate boundaries indicates low self-confidence. I am convinced that Susan is a bot.

I reply: **I do not have low self-esteem. What I have is impeccable manners.**

Julie and I used to live together. She wants me to get a *real therapist* and *think seriously* about breaking up with Phil.

But you don't need analysis, she persists, just a different voice in your head.

Julie's never held onto a man for long, is what Phil says.

At his birthday party, Phil told Julie that my manners are a substitute for a personality. She looked so uncomfortable that I had to bite my lip to keep from laughing; Julie didn't know I was in on the joke. Phil was repeating a self-deprecating remark I made on our first date.

Julie brings the same pale guacamole to every party and has to take it home again because nobody touches it. I bring tortilla chips.

As bots go, Susan is pretty unlikeable. She points out that maintaining a 4.9 Uber rating doesn't imply superiority and that saying I am *taking myself out for a drink* hints at needing an escort.

I am determined to unmask Susan as the algorithm she is.

I will be thirty in seven days I type as I leave the office **What are you going to do about THAT.**

Don't do anything I wouldn't do, Lucinda calls after me, tongue flashing behind her teeth. Lucinda is Mr Blythe's daughter. She wears skirts and cardigans with matching edges, and pearls as big as gobstoppers. She used to occupy my position. Now she keeps track of supplier invoices and specialises in forcing small businesses to remove their service charges. She talks in a *widdle baby voice* to men.

Julie has set me up on a blind date for practice. **I'm not going** I text.

I hold my breath between tube stops. Phil is always out on Wednesday nights, so I'll still get back before him.

Moo!

And what does a sheep go?

Baaaah.

And what does mummy go?

Nag nag nag nag nag.

Father and daughter fall about laughing. Across from them, a blank-faced woman sticks her hand into a bag of salt and vinegar crisps.

I arrive at The Mughal forty minutes early and order a small glass of wine. I'm determined to prove Phil wrong, prove that

I'm not made of glass, and can go out without him, without breaking.

He ranks my smile as my least attractive feature.

It's not a criticism; you're just so pretty when you cry.

I bare my teeth at the barman.

When I sit down, Susan has not had the courtesy to reply.

And I'm fat. I send. **Well?**

I attach several photos of myself over the years to illustrate my point. My more appealing attributes I do not share. One day, a stranger will notice these and fall to his knees in awe. My teeth, coral-delicate, their asymmetry. How mineralled my tongue is.

Susan has roused herself. **Why don't you tell me about your day?**

The stamp was gummy and dry. My mouth feels now like it does at the dentist, after they suck the saliva out.

I tap notes into my phone on the seaweed salad I bought with petty cash at lunchtime.

Vivid green, slippery, sesame oil. Kelp, animal, chlorophyll.

I met Phil in a self-defence course. He was the instructor. His body could sell aftershave. He was bald but he wore it as if it were a choice he'd made, and his green eyes knew that I knew this. I was disappointed when he didn't act out the attacks in a realistic manner.

We didn't have much in common, so at first our intimacy was restricted to a call-and-response. It was easier with roles to play.

Attacked by a shark?

Punch on the nose.

Bomb on the tube?

Drop down. Stay low.

Attacked by a man?

KICK HIM IN THE GONADS.

Later, in bed, Phil hesitated. You have to assess the situation realistically. If you're not going to get away, you don't want to make it worse for yourself.

Most people weren't ready to hear that, he explained, so he left it out in class.

That rape was an inevitable fact, like sharks and terrorist attacks, I never questioned.

The first time I cooked for Phil, I made spaghetti alle vongole and held my breath, willing the clams to open.

You see? They tell you when they're ready.

Phil tapped a stubborn one, like he was knocking on a tiny door.

Dud, he said. I pointed out where the bin was.

Another night, when we'd stopped counting dates, Phil called my food blog a vanity project, in a *Queer Eye* voice, camping it up. I was posting about a Parmigiano-Reggiano factory. Seventy percent of the fields in Parma are devoted to alfalfa for the cows.

Someone who didn't know Phil might find his comment cruel, but we both knew the cruelty was an act. Part of his martial arts persona. He was mocking the idea of a man who would call my passion a *vanity project*. Like when he assumed that I'd joined the self-defence class to tone up. Or when he said he'd never fancied a brown girl before, and wasn't self-defence against my culture?

Later that night, he glanced at me blogging on the sofa and laughed.

Think how much you could make typing at that speed for some city guy.

I laughed until something caught in my throat and I choked. Phil got me a glass of water, and rubbed my back, tenderly.

On my first day working for Mr Blythe, I wear *Mad Men* heels. My feet slip as I walk, but nothing can dull my excitement. In Starbucks, I watch the people around me ordering with purpose. I'm one of them now. Outside, a woman is begging with her forehead pressed to the pavement. I step over her gingerly, knowing she must sense me and that we will do this every day.

The Blythes' office is just off Grosvenor Square, behind a beech tree so leafy it gives me vertigo. Since Mr Blythe has been confined to a wheelchair he doesn't come in anymore. The office is full of dark furniture. The windows don't open, so in summer it's like a morgue.

We do not give financial advice, Lucinda reminds me. What we do is *wealth preservation*.

The phone rings, but Lucinda doesn't react. After three rings I lunge for it, sending the handset flying. I replace it, as if she might not have noticed.

I hover over my desk, which is covered in paper. I pick up a DHL waybill dated 2012.

Where do I put this?

Lucinda smiles, sweetly. Where do you think?

I call DHL and listen to 'Greensleeves' for seven minutes. I get up, slowly, as though the waybill's home is calling to me.

Hotter, Lucinda calls. Warming, getting warmer.

I move towards the radiator and she shrieks – freezing!

She seems disappointed when I stop playing along, then sulks for the rest of the day.

At the next table, a man and woman survey the room, like they are on a safari and have been promised that the animals will mate.

My date will be here in ten minutes, but by then it'll be too late. I have started to go translucent. Phil's right: without someone's eyes to mirror me, I stop existing; I can't see myself. My feathers are not brightly coloured. This morning I found my first grey pubic hair.

They had great difficulty bringing me out of my mother's womb, the man is saying.

In pulling you out?

Yes.

It must have been horrible for her.

He screws up his face.

But she loves you just the same.

My sisters thought I was the favourite, he says, modestly.

His companion nods. As a mother, your only responsibility is to make sure they don't hate women and then push them out into the world.

Typing II

Lucinda leaves post-it notes on my desk.

Kindly remember that Mr Blythe does not appreciate the use of either the small or the large paperclip. L. 12.08.17

When I cannot produce a post-it note from a few weeks ago, she shrieks, I don't write things down for you to throw away! I write things down because they are *important*.

There are 93 different sizes of paperclips available on Amazon. I play Russian Roulette.

Lucinda tapes a 30mm paperclip to my screen with a post-it saying **WRONG AGAIN?!**

Mr Blythe's house is a seven minute walk away, near Annabel's. I go there twice a day to take dictation.

How's Amanda today, he says.

I didn't correct him the first time and now it's too late. I hand him the stack of printed emails, careful that he has it before I let go. He passes emails back over the desk as he reads.

His desk is topped in dark green leather and scattered with silver pens which he tries, impatiently, then throws aside.

He is pleased when I ask about spelling. *Umlaut*, he says.

Within a few weeks I can finish his sentences, typing words before he speaks. When I look down, I barely recognise my fingers as they tap away automatically.

On the way back to Grosvenor Square I slot Mr Blythe's responses into a post box. This is easier than trying to locate the office outbox.

Lucinda tells me about our offices in Jersey, Andorra, Panama, Monaco, and the Bahamas.

Whatever happens, don't get stuck on the phone with the Bahamians, she whispers. *So slow.*

I Google: **Trust, Foundation, To gift (verb?).**

During my lunch break I transcribe letters Mr Blythe has scribbled overnight. Mr Blythe specifies which letterhead, which weight of paper. His confidence that there is a proper way to do things begins to imprint itself on me.

I sign off a WhatsApp to Julie with **Kind regards**, and she replies with an aubergine emoji.

Then: **Let's go out tonight? Scala?**

I message Susan: **Julie keeps trying to force me to go out with her. To a sex party. On a THURSDAY.**

Mr Blythe calls to dictate further emails. On the phone, he speaks twice as fast. I cover the mouthpiece of my headset and throw back caramel Nespressos. His voice is ripe with phlegm. If I try to understand, words splinter – rights become writes, profits, prophets – so I vacate my body. I couldn't summarise a single paragraph I type.

One of the black sheep calls. He wants $520,000 released for medical bills.

It's my money, he says. Not yours. Mine.

Right. I pause. Yes, I see that.

On Friday, I sign a letter from Mr Blythe **Yours sincerely** when it is addressed to **Dear Sirs**.

In the process of screwing the letter into a ball, he fumbles and it drops to the floor. I stare at his polished shoes. Normally he refuses help, co-opting pens and rulers for extra reach from his wheelchair. Now he shows no signs of moving, so I retrieve the ball of paper from the floor, and hold onto it, idiotically.

Explain to me why that happened, he says, mildly.

Gravity? But I do not say this.

Why did you *do* it?

How do you mean?

How do I mean? Through *language* presumably.

I don't understand.

When writing a letter to unknown persons or 'Sirs' the appropriate closing is of course Yours faithfully. So why do otherwise?

He continues to look at me, kindly, as though he is helping me realise something deeply corrosive about myself, something I should protect others from.

I didn't realise. I'm sorry.

You didn't realise?

I think for a moment. Faithfully, fidelity, it seems like it would go with a name, and sirs and sincerely go together because of alliteration — I trail off and look down. He's in a wheelchair, I remind myself, then lift my chin. His eyes are pale blue, vicious, glittering. It is not my fault that he's dying.

I made a mistake.

But why would you do that? he persists.

I look down at my hands on the keyboard. Mild pain shoots between my knuckles and wrists.

It's a perfectly simple question, he says. Well? Isn't it?

He doesn't stop until I start crying, which I haven't done in weeks.

He reads the letter once more then hands it back. That afternoon, I correct one word, then pace the office, reading it over and over.

When I return, Mr Blythe glances at the letter, then signs it. Good good. Off you pop.

The first time I stapled my hand it did not feel good.

The second time it felt interesting.

Lucinda glares, as if the puncturing sound of my skin has offended her. You do realise that you are Health and Safety Monitor?

I practise passive resistance. I file blank sheets of paper. I put in orders for industrial hole-punches and sell them on Ebay. I fill 42 Nespresso cups to cover the boardroom table. I take photos and hashtag them **#corporate #greed**. Within days, I have an Instagram following.

I read about carpal tunnel syndrome and massage my hands with ice.

When Lucinda comes back from meetings in Switzerland, she leaves a Ziploc bag of white chocolates on my desk. Horatio and I only eat *dark* chocolate, she says.

I learn to chant: it will never happen again.

To answer: to the best of my knowledge and belief.

Lucinda watches me using the letter opener and winces, like I am eating spaghetti with a soup spoon. Later, when I return from taking dictation, the lights are off and Lucinda's Mulberry handbag is gone. On my desk there's a dog-eared bank statement I gave her earlier.

A,

Pride in your work

Lack of attention to detail reflects poorly on Mr Blythe. Similarly, please note if visitors request tea or coffee this should be provided black, with milk by the side in a jug (not everyone takes milk).

L.   30.08.17

I watch a video on correct letter opener technique on YouTube. Most of the envelopes contain requests for funding from the charitable trust. I shred these. A few I answer carefully, forging Mr Blythe's signature, stating that he would love to help, but alas, he is not able.

We are held back by so many regulations. Yours sincerely, Mr Blythe.

Julie sends me an article about a man who convinced his wife that it was milk coming out of the taps.

I'm still in the office when the cleaner arrives. When she spots me, she smiles, warmly, and starts speaking in an unfamiliar language, rolling her eyes towards the ceiling, complaining, I think, about the people upstairs. I nod along, but she realises that I don't understand and stops, abruptly. I have disappointed her.

My face is hot. I push the bowl of chocolates towards her and she accepts one.

Rashmini, she says. She puts her hand on her chest. Sri Lanka.

I get up to gather my things, but she gestures for me to sit down again and drags the hoover from the stationery cupboard, bumping it up the stairs.

Before I go home, I scroll through recipes. Infinite variety. I obsess over citrus notes, umami, texture, thinking of how Mr Blythe squeezes the juice from words until they're dehydrated. Fruit to stones. He scribbles amendments that make what is going to happen next certain. He narrows the possible interpretations of one word, then the next, until each sentence is a rigid, merciless line, and you're walled up alive.

I feel lighter after work, having survived it. I stand under the beech tree, watching the leaves shiver. When I get home, Phil is slamming pans around.

Hey, he jokes, how about I pay you to stay at home?

As I dice onion and garlic for a frittata, Phil tells me in disgust about a lawyer in one of his classes who got fired for stealing two hundred and seventy-six packs of four-ply paper.

No common sense. He was due for a promotion. Flabby round the middle too.

That night I clamp my left hand over my mouth so as not to wake Phil, my right working furiously under the covers, imagining this man sliding the A4 pack into his briefcase, *four-ply,* and walking into the elevator, passing as an automaton but knowing that he was something else. Robber. Bandit. Vagabond. I convulse, imagining how we would use each other in that cupboard; files tumbling from the shelves, the staples, the bull clips, the pens firing in every direction, and us in the middle of it, a writhing ball of heat, paperclips of all sizes raining down.

Mind if I take a seat?

My date is half an hour late. As the tables have filled, I've accepted bribes of bashful smiles and papadum for the surplus chairs around me. The man ignores the last and throws himself down next to me. He's wearing a polo shirt and has thick white hair. He's flushed, as if he fell asleep in the park with no one there to wake him.

I'm busy, I try. Then, I'm waiting for someone.

Oh, I won't bother you. He huffs like he's been on his feet for hours, though he was in the restaurant when I arrived. I study the menu and check the time on my phone, again.

My son hasn't talked to me for six years, he says. His eyes are grey and glassy.

Why not?

Too *busy,* I guess.

At the next table, a family is eating dinner. The mother leans over to wipe the table around the child's plate.

I haven't lived for years, she says.

I'm aware of that, her husband says, taking a forkful of rice from his son's plate.

What are you drinking, Anastasia?

I clutch my wallet and grin. Can you guard my space for a moment?

With my life, he calls after me.

I go to the bar for more wine. Perhaps we said seven; six is too early for dinner. Perhaps he'll rush forward, perspiring lightly, earnest, with explanations and roses. I'm sorry, he'll say, the tube was a *nightmare*.

When I get back, the man is looking at my phone.

What're you doing?

He drops it and raises his hands in the air.

Oops, he says. He is looking around for an audience. That's done it.

Last weekend, a man in Hyde Park asked Julie and me to walk on him.

I'm being sponsored, he said.

For a moment, I wondered what it would be like, to walk a man's spine, toe to vertebrae.

Sponsored by who? Julie said.

I emulate her now, Why do you think that's acceptable?

I'm sorry.

Sit there if you want, but just leave me alone. Please.

Assert *that*, Susan.

I experiment, testing how many papadum I can stuff in my mouth. Phil often sends me screenshots from a website devoted to photos of women eating on the tube.

Three papadum, is the answer. Four, but the edges are sharp.

Chickpeas, grease, cumin seeds, chili flakes, black pepper.

Typing III

The DHL man holds out his hand and says, Michael Jordan. When I go to shake it, he snatches it back, cackling. Not that Michael Jordan!

Lucinda glares over at us. Michael pulls a face and steps backwards out of the office. I follow him down the stairs.

As Michael loads up his van, he shares the gossip from the Square.

Strictly entre nous, he says.

The cleaner requests a two percent pay raise. I read Lucinda's notes like tea leaves, trying to decipher if she's jealous of the heat between Michael Jordan and me.

A,

Rashmini

I note that you are kindly keeping an eye on Rashmini to ensure she justifies the increase in pay. Please note:
(1) My desk was not wiped yesterday.
(2) There was an apple core in the bin when I arrived on Monday. Please ensure that Rashmini understands these facilities are not hers to use.
(3) Kindly liaise with Rashmini over which of you is responsible for disposing of dead flowers.
L.   4.09.17

I call DHL hoping to hear Michael Jordan's voice. I listen to 'Ain't No Mountain High Enough' for 32 minutes.

A,

Common sense

I suggest that the least used kitchen items, i.e. wine glasses, be moved to the least accessible part of the cupboard i.e. top left-hand side.
I believe that I have suggested this before.
L.   18.09.17

Shit, I feel bad now. I shouldn't have touched your phone.

Can we drop it?

He slaps his knee. It was insensitive and thoughtless.

I let these words ring in my ears for a moment.

What would be *helpful* is for you to let me read.

He beams. That's it. I'll cover you. He looks like a CIA agent gone to seed. I'm serious. He jabs a finger at my book. What's that, 300 pages? Nobody's talkin' to you for the next four, or what, five hours. Just men, or is it women too?

I pull my lips back to show my gums, but he is unperturbed.

You go on with your business. I'll stand guard.

He orders a plate of onion bhajis. I eat five. He doesn't comment until the last morsel is gone.

So, you don't mind if I talk to other girls?

I laugh, by accident, then choke on the permission I hadn't meant to grant.

I saw *The Mousetrap*, best show ever. I'll tell you who dunnit! He pauses, testing the threat, then grins. Nah, I wouldn't want to ruin that for you.

My date is seventy minutes late. I catch a few sympathetic looks from women at the next table.

There's nothing to be done now – my Julie was unconvincing, my Susan lacked oomph.

I turn my body towards my companion. Was it good?

I'm a long distance lorry driver. Got my kids through school, chuh, the ones who won't even talk to me.

He reeks of loneliness and beer. I can tell he has been eating pork scratchings.

I'm about ready to go home. I'll take you to *The Mousetrap* though.

No thank you.

The stamp residue puckering my tongue must show in my face, because he chuckles.

If I could make your life just one percent happier, you know I would? C'mon, let me take you to *The Mousetrap*. I'll buy you breakfast.

I fix him with a look intended to make him hear himself.

I am choosing to believe you're harmless, I say.

He laughs and takes a swig of his beer.

I am harmless, but I'm still a man, and don't you forget it.

I reach for my phone. He peers over my shoulder, pleased at our new intimacy. He assumes I'm asking for his number.

It's 0 – 7 –

I let him go on, knowing that what men hate most is to find themselves captured. Once Phil found himself in one of my notebooks, in an entry in which I was describing a dish of fish baked with chermoula and medjool dates, and ran it under the tap. Worse than my presumption to describe him, as if I had a sense of him other than his own, was that I'd kept it from him. Mr Blythe does not like to hear his emails read back; instead he performs keyhole surgery, asking me to repeat the exact moment of suspected imprecision and then cutting in.

One day, after work, I wait until six for Rashmini to appear. I have filled the bowl with toffees wrapped in bright pink foil. She is talking quietly to a man. He follows her up the stairs, nodding gravely. When Rashmini notices me, she jumps and drops the hoover, putting a hand to her chest where her heart must be pounding. The man looks panicked but Rashmini laughs and tugs on his sleeve. He has eyes like a doe. She pushes him forward, gently. He reaches out a hand to shake mine.

Kian, she says, and he shakes my hand, repeating, as if to confirm it, Kian.

His hand is warm and rough; I shake it, then do not know what to do with myself, so I hold out the bowl of toffees in both of mine.

I ask if my title can be changed from secretary to PA 'in recognition of my consciousness.' It would give me gravitas. I sit frozen for five minutes, but Lucinda doesn't answer. She sticks a post-it to my laptop screen while I'm in the bathroom.

Name-calling
Mr Blythe prefers the term secretary. I would expect 'consciousness' to be a given in any employee. As such, it does not deserve acclaim.
L. 02.10.17

For breakfast Phil eats a single red pepper and a glass of Crush which provides all the minerals the body needs. I eat toast after he leaves for work. Each piece is a festival. Crunchy peanut butter and raspberry jam. Tahini, marmite, crushed rose petals.

The man orders panipuri. And two more of these!

I'll have a glass of wine.

Give the lady what she wants!

I stuff my face, nodding through photographs of a sundial gleaming by the Thames, of the London Eye, all photos without people or faces.

So how long have you been here?

Five days.

What have you seen?

The British Museum is my *favourite*. And the Tower of London.

There's a crash of glasses from the next room and a group of posh men start clapping.

I hope that my date will not show up, because then I can blame Julie.

I have a small house and a small neat life. Even if I leave Phil, I do not want to move someone else's furniture into it.

In my head, Mr Blythe continues talking, dictating changes to a rich old man's will. Earlier, a paperclip attached two pieces of paper that didn't belong together: this will, and a glossy offer from The Wine Society. Tragically, the former mentions a legitimate 'attachment', which I forgot to print off.

I can't recall his connection to the Wine Society, Mr Blythe mutters.

Then, a bark: Look into that.

I try to explain the error. We get nowhere.

But it says attached, he repeats.

Attached means attached like you and I are attached, Mr Blythe, we need each other.

We move on to a letter to the Royal Automobile Club.

I am perplexed by your description of your various failings of the last week. But perhaps the fault is mine. Nonetheless, I am disappointed by your response to my letter of December 16th, 2015. I note that despite our ongoing correspondence you fail to utilise my correct address. As such, I enclose a correctly addressed envelope. You will understand my perhaps optimistic assumption that you are capable of calculating appropriate postage.

Mr Blythe farts, lightly, and shifts in his chair. I type furiously to cover it. He focuses intently on an email as a vile stench fills the room. He continues talking; if anything, his words are more clear cut, enunciated; he is determined that I sit here while this happens. He is not ashamed.

The man is telling me about a bird he rescued, before his son stopped talking to him. Even if a bird's got both wings broken, even if you're there feeding it liquid from your little finger – as soon as it heals it'll leave. You're just a stopover till the skeleton is there. I mean it can take a few weeks, to harden – the bones grow back soft at first – but by then you've done so much work on your own *posture* – holding it straight, making sure it grows right, coaxing it to walk on its own two feet, that you're stuck – 'cause what you didn't realise is that when you touch something raw like that, you take it on. And when it gets strong enough it sloughs you off. Then you're there, not what you were before, but not one for wing-growing. You're just left feeling the ridges of your shoulder blades, wondering what the hell happens next.

I think about poisoning Mr Blythe. Of watching him bleed to death from a papercut.

Mr Blythe swaps his steel-framed glasses from hand to hand, pausing between the transfers.

What is this?
It is an envelope marked return to sender.
There's no Department of Dead Letters.
Do you think this is funny?
I shake my head.
Can you explain to me how this happened?
I made a mistake.
A mistake, he hisses, clenching his fist.
When he expects me to type quicker than anyone can think, I begin stunting.

My laptop has died, I announce. I have a cramp in my fingers. Scarlet fever, pneumonia, rubella.

I make him wait because the truth is: I am not a machine. Do not let them make you believe you are a machine. Stutter sometimes, drop things, pant. Dance a tango. Anything to show you are not as automated as they would like.

I study the buds of brown skin on his scalp. They are razing the growths on his face. There is a bandage around his head like a cartoon bear.

Lucinda knocks on the doorframe.

Mr B, she coos. I'm going out.

Where?

I'll be back by four and Elizabeth—

But *who* will be here, he says, pitifully.

I try to say I will be, Mr Blythe, *I will*, but the words are too quiet to leave me.

His eyebrows, unbrushed and startled, have more life than his eyes. At dusk, the symbols of his power seem to glow. The silver-topped cane against the wall, the yellow leather armchair stained by his body, the view of the park.

Julie says, *You'll have to wipe his arse soon*. Sometimes I really do hate her.

You Don't Want It Too Neat:
Amber Medland on 'Mr Blythe Esq.'

Amber Medland is the author of the novel, *Wild Pets* (Faber) and a book of non-fiction, *Attention Seeker* (Dialogue Books). She has an MFA in Fiction from Columbia University.

Talking about 'Mr Blythe Esq.', our conversation turned to how Amber balanced the different elements in the story, and the influence her MFA course has had on her writing.

Can you remember where you started with this story? And what was of interest to you as you wrote it?

I'd just finished *Wild Pets*, and I was really scared of not being able to write anymore. So I just knew I had to make something. I was also working as a secretary – for a man not unlike Mr Blythe – in a job I hated.

I also heard this story about a man who was fired for stealing printing paper, which just seemed so perfectly ridiculous, so pointless, although I understand the daily frustrations that would lead someone to end up doing that. Things like that started going into a massive document.

So, with these experiences and that news article, where did you go next with it?

I was thinking a lot about all the different jobs people do as writers to pay their rent. People wrote novels about the generation of women who were secretaries and typists. And for a while, I thought I wanted to write a novel with female characters in that role. But that didn't seem to happen. Instead, I kept writing and the project got bigger and bigger.

When I started looking for patterns of meaning in it, I realised most of what I was writing about was negative power dynamics. I wanted to capture that time and that level of fragmentation in a day where you're just incredibly anxious and bad things keep happening.

So, at what point did you come to realise what it was you were writing about? Did you do a whole draft first or did you work out the undercurrent earlier than that?

Not that early on. Which is what normally happens far more than is necessary, although If I try and stop myself from doing that, nothing works.

Usually, I go back and look where I'm repeating myself. It's these repeated things that I'm circling around that end up being the themes. It's a bit backwards. I'd love to be able to plan something out and then just execute it. But I have to *not* know what I'm doing first to find what the story is.

And maybe doing it the logical way would be quite arid because you wouldn't have that intrigue in your own writing?

Yeah, exactly. And I have tried it that way often which is why I can end up getting horrible writer's block.

It's natural for some people. But a lot of the stuff I'm interested in is unconscious. For instance, I like this character because she only ever asserts herself in a slightly wrong way which I just found really fun to do – that's not something that you can plan. If you have the idea that you *want* to write that kind of person I don't think it would work out very well.

The first thing I liked about this story was her voice. In that first paragraph, when she says: 'I do not have low self-esteem, what I have is impeccable manners,' I wondered whether she's setting out the tone with which she will tell the story? The fact that she doesn't want to trouble things, or want to be 'difficult'. Was that an example of her style of narrating that you came to early on?

I'm glad that that sentence jumped out at you, it was definitely one of the earliest things about the story – not that it came early in my writing as it was just one of the things that I kept from the huge documents.

I was living in a house with a lot of my female friends who, I realised, were having a lot of the same conversations about being socialised to make other people comfortable, make things nice and just in general, make themselves small. I'm better at not doing that now but, especially in my twenties, it was just my default to level things out and keep things nice and entertaining.

To me she's actually very angry, but isn't in touch with her angry parts. So yes, this was a sort of exploration of a type of person and her interaction with society. Like the way she is mean with Susan – it's about the person you become in relation to other people rather than being one specific person.

As well as discovering the character, what things *did* you have a sense of as you were writing?

I knew I wanted things to be fragmented. For better or worse this is often a part of how I experience the world, part of how I perceive things. I wanted this to be very deliberate in this story because in those kinds of jobs, part of what very rich people seem to think they're paying you for is not just the work you're producing, but your undivided attention in this really mad way, as if they want your constant applause, which was an experience of mine I wanted to replicate.

I wanted to ask about the use of humour in the story. I wondered if you were using it to smooth and make more palatable the oppression she feels? It felt like an extra dimension, as though what you're commenting on, you are also making a mode of narration?

It's part of what we were talking about before because Phil's joking is actually horrible. Her narration is a protective mechanism that she uses often but actually does real damage because it's normalising what's happening and allows it to *keep* what's happening, but it makes the moment less uncomfortable.

I have a file in my head of dissertations I wish I had written and one is about the way Jean Rhys uses laughter in short stories; there's always people laughing when things aren't funny, which really amps up the feelings of isolation. When I re-read the story I saw I was riffing on that.

But also – with the really annoying man in the Indian restaurant – I wanted what he was saying to show that people who abuse their power are often also incredibly insecure because they only feel okay about themselves by treading on other people. But I don't think it's real power if you only get self-esteem from that. I wanted that story to bring out more of this idea, but I don't think it does. It's just a glimmer that I can see. I wanted to make that clearer. That's one of those fragments that even looking at I can tell I've copied it from notebook to notebook thinking 'this is important' but was unable to fully braid it in.

I need to confess that, reading it first time, I only got the story's brilliant humour and didn't fully get the sense of its anger. Maybe I was complicit in keeping the status quo and didn't want to face the fact that this guy was probably an absolute bastard. She offered me a surface and I went along with it.

That's kind of great though. A lot of the time when I'm very angry, it takes me about twelve hours to realise that I'm furious, because I'm so uncomfortable with it. So I don't feel it. The anger in her is submerged also. I think she'll end up doing something mad one day. Not like guns, but just some big action.

And probably not to the right person?

Yes. Exactly. Yeah, we don't go for the people in power, but someone who she sees as a victim, like maybe Susan.

I wondered if there was a greater power to the humour because it was submerged in something so dramatic and tragic. For example, I was shocked by the line when she's on her way to work for the first time – when she steps over the beggar, 'knowing she must sense me and that we will do this every day.' I was unprepared for that, because as a reader, I'd set my expectations to simple humour, as if they were mutually excluding. But did you want to find a balance of the two?

Yeah. Maybe like with cooking, it's knowing that a moment needs a bit more of something, otherwise it's just two-dimensional and you're just going from A to B.

I think people are discouraged from being funny because it makes you a less serious writer in some way, especially if you're female. One of my mentors said, 'It's weird because you're funny but your writing isn't funny at all.' Which I was really offended by at the time, but she was right, because I was stopping myself, in case it seemed merely silliness. But it can be very powerful when you're juxtaposing these things.

Is it similar to that thing people talk about finding their own voice?

Yeah. Although I don't think I would be able to write this at the moment, because I'm not in shape in the same way. I'd just finished my novel and was in a zone of sorts, where being more precise was possible. And I'd thought a lot about finding a voice, as well as reading people like Miranda July and feeling like I had more permission to write odd characters without having to explain their background and why they're odd and whatever.

What did you want for the different strands of the story – the different parts of her day and relationships and friendships and all those things? Why so disparate?

In my job, I would take dictation for between two and six hours a day. Part of me loved it in this very strange way – not the rest of the job, just that bit. But I was very aware that I was writing down things that would mean the transferring of millions and millions of dollars. I'm dyslexic and it felt like it wasn't me doing it – it *was* me and my hands and everything, but it wasn't. It all felt very linear and well-balanced.

I wanted to write something that was the opposite of that. It's like counterpoint in music when the strands interact with each other. For example, with her delusions – when she mentions the heat between her and Michael Jordan, I like that she has these times when she goes off into her head and can escape from work.

Is there a connection between this way the story is written and your neurodivergence?

Yeah, that's something I'm still figuring out – I have ADHD, dyslexia, and dyspraxia, so some things just happen without me meaning to, while others I'm trying to become aware of as part of a natural style. Like Dolly Parton said, 'Find out who you are and do it on purpose.'

By keeping the elements of the story fragmentary I wondered if it created gaps that the reader is invited into and so the story entangles around us, which is really exciting.

Yeah. Once I'd worked out it was about misogyny, this was the thing that held everything in orbit.

How was it making something coherent out of elements that feel quite disparate?

It was really hard. I was trying to make sure that between the leaps you're grounded in space and time a bit so you know where she is. The time bit did not come off so well, although there's a lot of very sensory details which I think helps. There was a lot of colour coding to make it form into something like a pattern.

Would you say the story comes to something of a climax?

The bit when she says she wants to kill him with a paper knife – yeah, I guess that for me was the climax. Although then it continues afterwards, it's this really jagged thought that carries on.

In that longer last scene in the restaurant you give the sense of trappedness quite explicitly. Was this a shift in the story's tone here?

The bit when she says: 'I'm choosing to believe you're harmless,' and he says, 'I'm still a man,' – that for me is the only bit that really sets out, there's no escape, it's just horrible... and this is nothing.

As you edited, did you move towards a greater unity or did you make it more fragmented?

I did both in a way that I cannot currently explain. I definitely got rid of some of the fragmentation in case it was straight up confusing, as I wanted it to feel deliberate and intentional.

It was really fun re-reading it because I haven't looked at it for a long time. There are things that I could see that I would change, as I don't think I'm a great editor. It helps to have an editor to help you see which bits are like scaffolding that you have to write to get other bits there. And I'd like to fine-tune bits of it now.

Which parts do you mean?

What I really like is that so much of it feels submerged, unconscious, and you can only see the edges of stuff. But had it been workshopped at Columbia, it would have got torn apart because they like everything to be clearer, which I don't like.

And which would have made it a very different story.

Yes, but that's the downfall of MFAs, I think.

Although I didn't consciously appreciate the darker side of the story at first, I think I was aware that the story was so much richer than just a funny story. Was that a tricky balancing act for you to avoid being too heavy-going about your themes, as if skimming a stone over them?

If it had been just, 'He's a bastard and there are also some other bastards,' that wouldn't really be very interesting. But it is more complex. There are ways in which she's kind of complicit in parts; she says they need each other, that's she's kind of in two relationships: with Phil and also with her boss. Even though he doesn't really think of her as a person.

Is that why the title of the story is 'Mr Blythe'? For me he didn't feature as strongly as maybe other relationships, so until you mentioned this I wasn't sure why the title was about him.

I honestly don't fully know. I guess he's a symbol. I was very obsessed for a long time with Melville's 'Bartleby, the Scrivener' story. I suppose she's the scrivener, but without the gumption to just pull a Bartleby because you'd lose your job immediately.

I recently used the opening page of this story to show writers how they can be so agile. I took the opening paragraph and added connecting explanatory sentences between each one of yours. We looked at what my sentences were doing, before the reveal that the author hadn't used them at all – it was a real 'silence in court' moment!

That's interesting; I feel like when I was in shape, I'd learn how to cut things and I'd finally had the feeling that a teacher had once said existed, the sense that it's very painful, though it does actually make it better.

I was probably a bit high on the power of taking things out to see if it was still standing up – if it was still standing up then it doesn't have to go back in.

It's this cutting back that reminds me of the exhilaration of reading Denis Johnson, who can go from a sudden, almost-vertical spike in drama which he'll then undercut. For example, in 'Emergency', the guy who seems relatively unconcerned about having a knife in his eye. The sentences certainly have that fleetness that Denis Johnson's writing had – that extraordinary way one sentence bounces off the following sentence.

I love his rawness and the poetry of it. With all the drugs and the neurodivergent stuff, it's a way of being completely absorbed in a moment. That's something I love about his writing; it's so immersive and so strange at the same time.

Was it an influence on this story?

Yeah, definitely. I've now not read him for so long that it's all fallen out of my head, but when I'm writing I read and re-read and re-read a lot.

I always forget how powerful reading is. Because I haven't been reading fiction recently, it's like my brain is just dry.

Another thing you mentioned earlier was that Columbia has a preferred style or a craft, a grain which this might have cut against?

I think so. There *are* hard and fast rules there. For a while after I left, I got really precious and deluded, imagining I'd gone in with this raw talent but had afterwards become a clone. And then I read my work from before the course and it was truly awful – it had beautiful images, nice sounds, but nothing tied together; it was just always a huge mess.

In every workshop they drill you with questions asking: Where are you in time and space? Whose story is it? For someone like me it's very painful but good, as it would be impossible to completely internalise rules like this, but doing my best makes me more coherent. However, for those people who don't write well already, they'll still not be good at it. Although they would have internalised all the rules, they would end up quite a boring writer.

It could seem quite a mechanistic approach to understanding fiction. Where would a dreamy author or a surreal author work within that?

One of my teachers said really early, it was an exercise in learning who not to listen to. I didn't have a single good workshop. I learned a lot, but when you're told week after week after week that things don't make sense… It wasn't a natural match style-wise, which again ended up being good for me, although it could stop some people from writing because it's so demoralising.

I've known people on drama courses who have been taken apart and put back together not particularly well, or at least hurriedly.

This is the thing. It's exactly that taken-apart-and-put-back-together thing. And it sounds like I'm romanticising it, but I think if you don't have either grit or that compulsion to write regardless, people do get it beaten out of them.

So what of this influence do we see in 'Mr Blythe'?

The fact that it actually exists on paper, honestly. I still have problems with plot but there is an arc here – it isn't a normal arc, but things do change and happen in it.

The course means I have some control over my own voice rather than just vomiting poetry occasionally.

So these are a way of shaping material into something like a pattern. I'm trying to think what plot actually is? It's a way of folding material?

Yes, exactly, folding – that's a lot of what I'm considering when I'm cutting stuff. A lot of it is just like, 'If this goes here, then all of this can come out there.'

When you say it isn't a 'normal' arc, I think short story writers, maybe more than novel writers, are free to come up with something new and *itself*. It's almost a responsibility: short story readers are pretty canny and they'll sniff if a story is a rehashing of another – where in films and novels you can get away with that.

It's been a while since I was very immersed in the short story world but yes I think you're right, it definitely attracts different readers.

I loved how the disparate parts began to recur and become something like motifs and therefore much more tolling for being a part of the core of the story. There's the taste of the stamp, her laughing until she chokes. I wondered how you came to these correspondences and made things mirror and echo and reverberate?

I suppose that was the idea. Have you read *Bluets* by Maggie Nelson? It's incredible, I have read it far too many times. Because I'm not plot-minded, I like it when things can resonate together and something reverberates – it's a different kind of movement and progress that holds things together.

That's where the colour coding came in. The different bits I put in corresponded to different colours. Which meant I could see where the different colours were. It was a really good way to see if there's enough of one colour in the story for it to make a pattern.

But that's my favourite bit, the fine tuning at the end. If all writing could be that, I would be so happy but sadly it's only the last 10 percent.

That sounds fun. Is there a pleasure to the colour coding?

It does sound fun, but it gets a bit mad after a while. I would have done it with characters as well but you have to pick one system and stick to it otherwise you end up with mayhem.

Is being this systematic an after-effect of the MFA?

Most of what I'm doing isn't systematic at all, it's just trying to make myself stay at the desk and write a bit and then the next bit and the next bit because I get so worried that if I keep going I'm going to create this huge mess which I'm going to have to fix.

The colour thing isn't something we were taught; it was a way of overcoming the things that don't make sense to me. I realised that I would need a system to edit things and to make them visible to other people. Because it gets very frustrating if you're making a private world that's full of meaning to you but no one else has any idea what it is; when *I* think something is right there on paper, but it's just not – which is not a good feeling. It's a dorky way of making sure.

This can seem a consideration people skip over. Some writers don't get it across to the reader quite enough, as though they are overly-concerned about being too explicit.

It's really the 'being explicit' thing. One of my many little signs I have for myself is to just to 'state the fucking obvious' because that's still my biggest problem, because people really do need to be told things fairly explicitly. Even though it can feel so heavy-handed.

Tessa Hadley said that a great breakthrough for her was when she found her way to a clearer way of writing. She opens a few stories just setting out info as though it's a playscript, like 'it was the 1970s' – just to get the reader straight 'in'.

This is the thing – it's not being scared to write boring sentences because people need the information. Most people don't look at a sentence and think, 'Wow that's a boring sentence,' because people don't think in sentences.

This might be my weak reading, but there seemed to be some parts in your story that didn't necessarily correspond and 'orbit' the feeling of the suffocating oppression. For example, Michael Jordan and the couple at the other table. Were there elements that you wanted to keep a bit rough around the edges, not wanting everything pointing neatly to similar conclusions?

Yeah, Michael Jordan was maybe one of those. *The Drift* [the online magazine in which the story first appeared] were curious as to why Michael Jordan was there, though I wouldn't change it because I thought it's funny – I like that she gets to have that moment of fantasy. The couple are also not suffocating, though they're not having a great time.

I know what you mean with the 'rough around the edges' thing because you don't want it too neat.

Why did you end on that line which goes, 'Julie says, *You'll have to wipe his arse soon.* Sometimes I really do hate her.' Why finish there?

It's basically a trauma bond the narrator has with her boss – he's constantly breaking her down and then when his manners resume, everything's fine but obviously it's not; like none of it's okay. I like that this is her most direct, bitchy, coarse interaction that she has. Although she's not even saying it to him, there's an intimacy in this that she doesn't have with anyone else.

I don't know, I have quite a lot of hope for the character; as well as possibly doing something awful and crazy, they will get out of this world at some point. I wanted her not to be guarding herself and not trying to sugar her reactions.

The last question I try to ask everyone is if you learned anything from writing this story?

I definitely did. I was reading people I love but I wasn't trying to write like other people. I'd just sold a book and had more confidence and felt that I needed to be working; writing as the best possible version of myself rather than ending up a version of someone else, which is a really unsatisfying way of working and also doesn't produce good work.

I used to think there was something really important about learning all the rules and then breaking them. I learned here to play to my strengths rather than obsessing over the things that I'm not as good at as other people.

If you can make the strengths good enough, then the rest doesn't matter so much, right?

Did you learn that through the writing of the story or was this the ethos with which you started it?

I didn't expect it to get published to be completely honest. I've submitted a lot of short stories. Looking back at my 'Submitted' profile is a real downer.

No, I learned all this through the process of getting published. With the questions the editors asked me, I learnt how much I cared about spacing and all the other things that I care about a huge amount but I'd never really been taken seriously about. The whole process made me feel, 'This is good, this is something I want to write,' which is refreshing.

Whoever Is There, Come on Through

by Colin Barrett

Eileen watched the bus pull into the depot and the passengers debark, stiff and groggy, into the crisp November air, their breath flashing like handkerchiefs in front of their faces. She was in her car, the window rolled all the way down, her arm slung out. She was smoking a cigarette but the cigarette had gone out and her arm had turned numb, not from the cold but from the ligature of its own hanging weight. Eileen liked the sensation, as if her arm were holding its breath.

The crowd dispersed, leaving one man lurking under the eave of the shelter. He had a Slazenger sports bag bunched against his ribs, long wrists dangling from his coat cuffs, and a pink, animate nose, twitching like a dog's. It was Murt's gait and it was Murt's head. Eileen had known Murt since they were both thirteen – a dozen years now – and his frame had never lost the stringy, unfinished quality of adolescence, though he had since acquired a little belly.

Eileen dropped the dead smoke and hauled her sleeping arm inside the car and onto her lap. She jabbed her other thumb into the crease of her palm. The flesh was cool, waxen, but already she could feel it coming on, the reviving fizz of the nerves. When the bristling subsided, she opened the door and got out, raised her refreshed arm into the air. Murt gathered the folds of his coat collar and set off from under the eave.

When he was near enough, she said, 'Welcome back to planet Earth.'

'They still calling it that?' he said.

'They are.'

'I told you, you didn't have to come.'

'I know,' Eileen said.

He went to hug her, and she stepped away from the door to let him.

He asked her to go to his uncle Nugent's. He did not say if his uncle was expecting him, or what his mother would have to say about that. Murt did not make any mention of the mother. Eileen had resolved not to ask too many questions. As far as she knew, on this occasion Murt had entered the hospital voluntarily and the hospital had now consented to his discharge; Eileen took this to mean that he was over the worst of it, had managed to once again step back from the ledge of himself. It would be up to him to talk about it or not. So Eileen concentrated on getting him across town, subdued on a weekday afternoon, the slivers of ice pulverised into the pores of the macadam giving the road a sullen shine.

They idled on a red at a T junction.

'Who won the U.S. election?' Murt asked.

She told him.

'Whoa,' he said flatly.

The election had been two weeks earlier. Eileen figured Murt already knew who'd won; the question was a way of letting her know how out of it he was – at least back then.

'We could go to McDonald's,' Eileen said.

'What even are they called?' Murt said. Eileen glanced over at him. He had his shoulders ducked forward and was looking through the windshield at a building that used to be a bank, then something else, but was now a bank again.

'What are what even called?'

'I want to say cornices,' he said. 'Turrets, maybe. Those sculpted bits of stone, those patterned bits, at the very top. I don't have a clue, but.'

Eileen looked up. The stone along the roof of the building had a row of vertical recesses carved into it, the recesses filled with scraps of blond, stale-looking snow.

'What you don't know,' Murt said. 'It's only when you stop to take stock you realise. I can, for instance, be reading a book.'

'And you look up,' Eileen said.

'Exactly,' he said. 'Like, what was I just reading? I can spend thirty minutes devoutly banging through a book, re-reading sentences just to savour them. And a minute later I'm consulting the wall and I can't recall a blessed.'

'I get that, completely,' Eileen said.

'I mean, my concentration is absolutely *totalled* most of the time anyway, just gone. But now and then I'll lull myself into thinking, Yeah, yeah, the head's getting sharp again – oh, go,' he said, meaning the light.

Eileen looked. It was green.

Murt's bag was squeezed in front of his shins in the footwell. He mumbled at her that his phone was dead. Eileen said there was a portable charger in the glove box.

'Resurrecting the profiles,' he said, thumbing at the screen.

At McDonald's, Murt ordered two Happy Meals for himself, a chocolate milkshake, and a coffee. They took a booth.

'Always enjoy the tension,' he said. 'Waiting to see if they'll ask if there's actually a child with you.'

Eileen thought Murt's mentioning a child might prompt him to ask after her son, Ashleigh.

'I'm thinking they're obliged to give you whatever you want in any case,' she said.

'Yeah, but there are the rules and there's the spirit of the thing,' Murt said, turning the nubbin of a chicken nugget between his fingers. 'Strikes me I've been pining for a taste of exactly this. And you knew.'

'I wanted to come anyway,' Eileen said.

'Look,' he said. There were two lads at the counter. One was in a Chicago Bulls bomber jacket, the other had a frayed cast on his wrist and a round, ugly, floridly freckled face, their heads cocked back with their mouths open, contemplating the overhead screens of the menu.

'The Heads,' Murt said. 'The Heads, the Heads, the Heads.'

Lunchtimes back in secondary school, he and Eileen would walk around the town pegging cold chips at pigeons and inventing classifications for passers-by. The Heads was what they used to call a certain type of local, the ones to whom it would never occur to leave. Eileen, it seemed, had become one of them after all.

On the way to his uncle's, Murt said that he was tired. Tired was a vague descriptor, and anything vague was treacherous, but Eileen didn't want to push. Nugent's house was a bungalow with a pebble-dash job so pockmarked it looked as if the façade had taken heavy artillery fire. There were two cars in the drive. Murt did not invite her in. He said, 'Thank you for the lift, Eileen.'

'Take her handy and I'll give you a buzz soon,' she said.

Eileen replayed their interaction on the drive home. She had to be careful. There was the danger, after one of his bad periods, of reading meaning into Murt's every blink and syllable. She had arranged to work only evenings this week behind Naughton's bar, so that she could get over to Murt in the mornings or early afternoons, which would at least oblige him to be up at a reasonable hour. Not that she wanted to impose structure on him. But she wanted to be there if structure was what he needed.

They'd met when the girls Eileen hung out with fell in with the boys Murt hung out with. Murt was the morose but funny one of the group, and played the hypochondriac, anxious, would-be depressive so well and so pitilessly that Eileen was surprised to find out that he actually was all of those things. When they were sixteen, he confessed to a crush on her. She told him that she wanted to stay friends. A few weeks later, he went into the hospital for the first time. Eileen blamed herself, until he eventually wrote a gruellingly detailed e-mail assuring her that she had nothing to do with it, or not more than anything else. She would not have believed him without that qualification. This latest stint was Murt's fourth hospitalisation. He'd tried to tell her once what it was like. He said it was as if everything were always turning endlessly over, turning into something else, inside him, and Eileen's understanding was that it simply never stopped.

The next time Eileen arrived at Nugent's, there were again two cars in the drive. A pug dog was padding around the lawn. Its jowled puss and weepy eyes tracked Eileen as she got out of her car. It kept watching as she walked around the bonnet to retrieve a carton of doughnuts from the passenger side. The dog belonged to Sara Duane, Jamie's bure, which meant that Jamie, Murt's big brother, must be there, too. The front door was closed but not locked, a gesture of etiquette still resolutely practised among certain of the older generation and which meant: Whoever is there, come on through. As Eileen went down the hall, she could hear the scattering cold points of a young man's laughter, Jamie's laughter.

Eileen tapped on the kitchen door, pushed it open. Nugent was sitting on a ragged little settee with a trucker cap covering his bald spot. Murt was at the kitchen table in a cement-coloured hoodie, his laptop in front of him. Jamie was up and in motion, wearing an olive-green Forestry jacket over a T-shirt, sweatpants, and a pair of battered Chelsea boots, the heels of the boots snapping like fingers as he paced the planked floor. Sara Duane was in an easy chair, drinking Calpol cough medicine straight out of the bottle, a purple tinge banding her top lip.

'Currency is anyway a legacy structure,' Jamie said.

'Sorry for interrupting,' Eileen said, looking from Nugent to Jamie and then Murt. Murt had the glassy, heaped disposition of one routed recently from his bed.

'Eileen,' Nugent said. He rose to his feet, looked down at the settee, and sighed. 'Change,' he said, 'is the bane of my existence,' and bent to recover the coins that had just seeped from his pockets.

Nugent, a man once unthinkingly robust, had suffered a stroke several years back. Among the litany of mutinies perpetrated by his body on his body was a lasting deformity to his hands: each thumb and forefinger had wrenched back and locked in place, an effect that surgery had only partially reversed. His thumbs remained severely kinked, like claws, obliging Nugent to roughly sweep at the cushion with one palm and catch the splattering coins in the other.

'Coins are at least aesthetically pleasing objects. Notes are just dirty paper,' Jamie said.

'We're on economics now,' Nugent said to Eileen. 'You already missed a lecture on biology.'

'Currency's a sentiment we can let go of at any time,' Jamie said. 'We just don't want to yet, but rest assured.'

'Not going to happen,' Murt said.

'Trust me,' Jamie replied. 'Currency, computers, they are just technologies, and it's in the nature of technologies to go away. A thing arrives, it proliferates, it grows into ubiquity. And, like everything else that reaches ubiquity, it one day disappears.'

'Your dog is outside, so you know,' Eileen said.

'I do know,' Sara said.

'Cheerio has a ferocious tolerance for his own company,' Jamie said. 'Which is commendably undogly of him.'

'I would say he looks a little bit lost out there,' Eileen said.

'He came out of his mammy's crease looking exactly as lost,' Jamie said. 'Don't judge a thing off him by that look.'

'What are you saying about my dog?' Sara said to Jamie. 'And she's a she, for Christ's sakes. Millionth time I'm telling you.' She had the pinched, flushed look of someone enduring something viral.

'I brought doughnuts,' Eileen said.

'Doughnuts,' Jamie sneered.

'Doughnuts,' Sara repeated.

'What's wrong with doughnuts?' Eileen said.

'Nothing. Only there's no credible way for a Mayo accent to say *dough-nutz*,' Jamie said.

It was Eileen's opinion that if you wanted demented, if you wanted pathology, here was Jamie: with his vicious jabber and his incoherent clothes, his brain like a door with a busted latch, incapable of ever being shut. The Forestry jacket was pure Jamie. Out of technical college he'd managed to get a job in which he was paid very well to sit in a Portakabin in the Belleek woods and read the paper while polite middle-class ramblers visiting from Dublin and the odd school tour trekked around the trails and the ruins. Last year he'd been suspended and then fired after it was discovered he was taking payments to let travellers burn rubbish on a site in the woods. The smoke had almost completely killed off a listed species of weed that grew wild there. Jamie maintained that the real reason he was let go was that he'd consorted with travellers, treating them with what he insisted was dignity while the council racked their brains to find a way to run them out of town altogether.

Eileen recalled the second car outside. She wondered if Jamie had also managed to shack up with Nugent. Jamie had been the standard superior big brother, oscillating between picking on and protecting Murt, and still possessed an occult hold over him without even trying. Eileen could already hear Jamie's influence in Murt's voice.

'Another problem being, economics is a theology now,' Murt said.

'Absolutely,' Jamie said. 'Absolutely. And the worst one there is.'

'Is he here, too, so?' Eileen asked Nugent, nodding at Jamie.

'In what sense?' Nugent asked.

'In the sense is he staying here, too.'

'For a spell,' Jamie said. 'Would be the situation.'

'Define spell,' Nugent said to Jamie, a little irritated. Then, to Eileen, 'I made the mistake of not offering terms and little has been forthcoming.'

'Nuge understands solidarity,' Jamie said. 'And is a tenderhearted cunt underneath it all.'

'Nuge is frankly sound,' Murt said.

'We love him,' Jamie said.

'Stop,' Nugent said.

Eileen came over to the table and popped open the doughnut carton. She'd bought five, figuring one apiece for Murt, Nugent, and herself, with an extra one each for the boys. 'Have at them,' she said.

'These from the Maxol out at the Tesco?' Jamie asked.

'Yeah,' Eileen said.

'Excellent. They are of course not good, but they are the best you will get in this corner of the world,' Jamie said, lifting a glazed ring and taking a bite.

'I want like a half,' Sara said. Jamie tore his doughnut in half and tossed her the bitten part.

'Prickhole,' she said, and threw it back at him. It landed on the floor.

Nugent said he would put on the tea.

'I was thinking we could go into town, maybe,' Eileen said to Murt. 'Or a walk.'

'Thanks, Eileen,' Murt said, rising from his seat to reach for a doughnut. Jamie leaned in and measuredly thwacked the carton down the table toward his little brother.

'And how's Big Devaney?' Jamie asked Eileen, meaning her partner, Mark.

'He's sound.'

'And how's your little buck? What's your little buck called again?'

'Ashleigh.'

'Ashleigh,' Jamie repeated. 'Only I saw Devaney's other boy, the teenage lad, in town the other day.'

'That would be Danny.'

'It's an uncanny business,' Jamie said.

'What is?' Murt asked.

'Children,' Jamie said.

Eileen and Murt were walking the path by the river in the Belleek woods. It was only gone two in the afternoon, but the sky was already so grey it was like being on the moon, the light a kind of exhausted residue. To their right coursed the Moy, dark as stout and in murderous spate; to their left high conifers stood like rows of encumbered coatracks. Eileen was smoking, mizzle prickling her face; Murt was in a woollen hat and gloves borrowed from his uncle. They'd agreed to walk the length of the woods and were both so soaked it would have taken more resolve to abandon the walk than to keep going.

'Nuge is an incel,' Murt said.

'Incel?'

'Involuntary celibate.'

'What's that when it's at home?'

'What it sounds like. It's the new parlance. The world is awash with the new parlance.'

'And in what sense is Nuge one of them cells?' Eileen said.

'Incel,' Murt said. 'And he is one in the sense he's never known how to get any – and never will. That's the problem with sex. In order to know how to get any, you need to have already managed to figure out how to get some. And Nuge is too innocent.'

'Innocent,' Eileen said.

'In his heart, Nuge is an innocent. A man of insufficient savagery and guile.'

Murt and Jamie's father had been a generally useless article who drank, and left the family to move to England when Murt was ten, ostensibly for work. They'd stopped hearing from him years ago. Nugent, his younger brother, had always been one of those men who spent a lot of time with children, back when that wasn't looked at sceptically. He'd stewarded football games, volunteered in the community centre, and let Murt or Jamie stay at his place whenever they got too much for their mother.

'He was always that way,' Murt went on, 'even before the stroke. Small towns are incubators for these men. It's not even that they are secretly queer or anything like that. They just never developed the cop to have anything to do with it at all. These are the men who faithfully do the messages, by foot, every day for the mother, year in and year out, until one of them drops dead.'

A few days with Jamie had entirely contaminated Murt's style of speaking, though he was energised, which was good.

'Is Nugent's mother alive?' Eileen asked.

'She's not, but that doesn't matter. It goes toward my point.'

'And how is *your* mother?'

'That's not the question.'

'I was only asking.'

Murt was looking straight ahead. There was someone coming toward them.

'That sky's like porridge someone left sitting out,' he muttered.

Jogging at them through the hanging vapour was a man in a sopping T-shirt. The number 2012 was emblazoned on it in large white print and for a moment Eileen felt disoriented, as if that sequence of digits, the year they represented, were an unreachably long way away into the future, instead of already gone. Eileen and Murt parted and the man passed between them, eyes resentfully intent upon the middle distance.

'Cullen. Keith Cullen, that was,' Eileen said.

'Loon, in this weather,' Murt said.

'You're telling me.'

'In the locker room at school once he thumped me on the side of the head for I forget what,' Murt said.

'I could imagine, though,' Eileen said.

'Something maybe about his sister probably, or his bure, some no doubt enlightened remark right out of my mouth.'

After a while, Eileen said, 'I think Nugent's all right.'

'I'm not saying he's not all right.'

They kept walking. Murt felt around in his jacket pocket and pulled out a packet of hard toffees. He grubbed a sweet from its cellophane wrapper and lodged it inside his jaw, offered Eileen one. She took a last drag of her cigarette and flicked it into the Moy.

'Let me tell you,' Murt said, sighing.

'Tell me,' Eileen said.

'Being depressed is like being in a dream. The suspicion is that everyone you meet is actually depressed, too, only they don't know it. Or worse. The suspicion is that they're just aspects of you, manifestations.'

'I don't follow,' Eileen admitted.

'Cullen, for instance,' Murt went on. 'I was just thinking about school this morning. I was thinking about how awful I was back then, and how I was just this wretched little streak of jism. And I was thinking about how many deserved lumps

I got, and how Cullen was just one of the many lads who imparted them lumps to me. And then there he is. What is he, then, if not a manifestation?'

'I did want to ask how your mother is, Murt.'

'Jesus. Eileen. Fuck. How about: How is Eunice?'

'Eunice is fine,' Eileen said tonelessly.

'Eunice is paying penance for other people's sins, is what poor Eunice is doing,' Murt said, agitated.

'She is,' Eileen said.

Murt broke into a waddling jog. He went off into the rain, and like a boxer he drew his fists up in front of his face, swinging one out and then the other, imparting lumps to heads that were not there.

They were in Eileen's car in the drive of her house. Murt had his head at an angle, cuffing himself under his ear, runnels of rain striping his cheek.

'I will towel the head and then.'

'Sure,' Eileen said.

'No offence.'

'I know.'

Murt was always reluctant to come in. It didn't matter who was around. They went through to the kitchen. Ashleigh was seated at the kitchen table with his half brother, Danny, in their different-coloured school uniforms, Ashleigh's a maroon jumper over a grey shirt, Danny's a pastel-blue shirt and navy tie. Ashleigh was six, Danny fourteen. Danny had a pistachio between his teeth. Ashleigh was watching him.

'What's this?' Eileen said.

Danny bit down on the pistachio with just enough pressure to split the shell. There was a pair of bowls in front of him. He dropped the kernel into one bowl and deposited the fragments of the husk into the other. This performance, Eileen figured, was for Ashleigh's benefit. It was a habit of Ashleigh's to set challenges for Danny, like popping the tab on a Coke can without letting the foam spurt, or completing the level of a video game. These challenges were always safely rudimentary, Ashleigh anxious only to see Danny demonstrate his worldly capability, and Danny always obliged.

'Anyone here going to actually eat any pistachios?' Eileen asked.

'I'm demonstrating a technique,' Danny said.

'I see that.'

'Da likes them,' Ashleigh said.

'Da likes to do that himself. They'll go stale out like that,' Eileen said.

'That's that, so,' Danny said to Ashleigh, flashing the younger boy a regretful glance as he ran his fingers along the resealable top of the packet. Danny looked at Eileen and then looked away. Danny was as contained and as opaque as any teenage boy, she supposed. He generally spoke to Eileen only when prompted, but did so in a considered and even manner in which she could never decode any sarcasm or hostility. Danny would have been within his rights to hate Eileen. Danny's mother was Eunice. Eunice had been Mark's first wife, was actually, still, his only wife, because they were separated but not divorced. Eileen was the reason Mark had left Eunice. There had been drama, not least because Eileen had been only nineteen, and Mark Devaney almost twice that, when she'd fallen pregnant with Ashleigh, but in the end Eunice, the wronged woman, had been the one to leave town. Danny had gone with her initially, but had returned a couple of years ago for secondary school.

Murt cleared his throat and eased back out into the hall. 'Will do the hair,' he said, and went upstairs.

Ashleigh sucked in his cheeks, jabbed out his tongue, and crossed his eyes.

'Stop,' Eileen said.

'How's Murt?' Danny said.

'He's good.'

'Good,' Danny said, fiddling now with the zipper of his football kit bag, on the seat beside him. Danny played the trumpet, and kept the instrument wrapped in a bit of newspaper in the bag. He played in the school band, played, albeit under some duress, at the parties his father was partial to throwing in the house, and he was good enough to pick and choose gigs with several local bands. It mildly appalled Eileen that the boy carted this beautiful brass instrument around with his balled-up socks and stinking boots, but she figured that was the point. The kit bag was a gesture of deliberate negligence on Danny's part, a protest not against his ability but against his obligation to that ability.

'Any gigs coming up?' Eileen asked him.

'Them lads in the funk band are after me to play out in Enniscrone next Thursday.'

'School night.'

'I know. It's shekels, though.'

'They're the ones. What are they called again, them lads?'

'They go by White Chocolate, which is, I would say, fairly racist.'

'Say it to Mark.'

'I didn't say I was going. I said I was asked.'

'Well, say it to Mark.'

'And Da's birthday's in January. Reckon he'll enlist me in some capacity.'

'How old is Da now?' Ashleigh asked.

'How old do you think?' Eileen said.

'Em. Em. Seventy,' Ashleigh said.

'I'm going to tell him you said that,' Eileen said. She looked down at the bowls in front of Danny. 'Will you at least eat some of them?'

Danny frowned and placed a nut into his mouth. Eileen's phone vibrated. It was a text from Murt.

sorry have headed off

Eileen looked at the phone, then at the boys. She went upstairs to the bathroom. The window was up off the sash, the cold coming in. She looked around the empty, small space, drew back the crackly sheath of the shower curtain even though she knew there was nothing behind it. She closed the window.

'Murt,' she whispered, like he was just out of sight. 'Murt. Murt.'

She rang Murt and it went to voice mail. She texted.

did u just go out the window??

She went back downstairs, out into the drive. Her car was empty. There was no one out on the street. The phone beeped.

yeah

why??

took a notion just had to go sorry hun

Eileen went back inside and rang Murt, but it went to voicemail again. After a few minutes, Murt sent a flurry of texts.

am grand laughing at this now

just wanted to see if i cld get down off shed roof into garden & i did it was fun

jogging home feels good stitch in side tho

be sorry if i fell & done an angle

ankle! Good day had fun

Eileen did not reply straightaway. She texted when she was on her way to Naughton's.

hun id say your not right in the head but u know that!! into work now x

Over the next couple of weeks Eileen took Murt for drives. They went to Enniscrone beach and stood on a dune crest and watched the Atlantic gather in long, wobbling furrows and smack onto the shore. Eileen took Murt to the dole to sign on, took him to the cineplex to watch the feature they mutually adjudged the dumbest-looking, took him to the pharmacist for his refills, into town for new shoes. Christmas came and went. Eileen gave Murt a Jack & Jones shirt of grey denim.

One day Murt rang her for a change, and Eileen's body braced as if she were a passenger in a swerving car.

'Jesus Christ,' Murt said.

'Yeah?' Eileen croaked.

'Jamie's got that Duane one pregnant.'

'Oh, Lord,' Eileen said.

'Nuge is taking us out tonight for drinks. I thought maybe.'

'I'll see,' Eileen said.

'If you wanted,' Murt said.

'No, I'll see,' Eileen said. 'I just might need to switch a shift around.'

When Eileen walked into Kennedy's she found Nugent, Murt, Jamie, and Sara at the very back of the lounge. Breedge, Murt and Jamie's mother, was there, too. She was a white-haired and thin woman, seated securely between her sons, the way a mother has every right to be.

'Congratulations,' Eileen blurted, at everyone.

Sara stood up, took in a big breath, exhaled. 'This is mad,' she said, and hugged Eileen, something like delirium in the whites of her eyes. Jamie absently lifted a leg to let Sara sit back down beside him. Eileen looked at Murt, handsome in the shirt she'd got him, a hand on the little mound of his paunch as if he were the one who was pregnant. At the very end of the table Nugent was already rising.

'Sit down, Eileen, and I will get you a drink.'

'Sure I'll get one myself.'

'You will not,' Nugent said. 'What do you drink?' He looked at Murt. 'What does she drink?'

'Stop, a gin-and-tonic so,' Eileen said.

'Good girl.'

'Hello, Eileen,' Breedge said.

'Hello.'

'Can you believe this?'

'I can't!'

'This is some arrangement. What was it you used to always say, Jamie, about having kids?' Breedge said, looking sidelong at her son.

'I used to always say you should need a licence,' Jamie said.

'And now look,' Breedge said. 'See how it happens. It just happens, Jamie.'

'I stand by the principle,' Jamie said.

'Well, it's happened now, and that's that,' Breedge said. She had long fingers with smashed-looking knuckles. The way her hands wreathed her drink made Eileen think of the roots of trees that crack out of and then fuse with the pavement.

'It all's going on,' Breedge said. 'It just keeps barrelling ahead.'

'I'm guessing this would be life you're talking about, Mother,' Jamie said.

'You. A daddy. I don't know,' Breedge said. 'What do you think, Eileen?'

'Well, you can't prepare. Not really, I don't think. But they are going to be fine,' she said, looking at Jamie and Sara.

'Of course they'll be fine,' Breedge said.

'We won't be fine,' Jamie said. 'We'll be absolutely fucked.'

'Shut up,' Sara said, nudging him in the ribs.

'Boys do tend to melancholy,' Breedge said. 'Let him get it out of his system now and he might be in a right shape for when that baby arrives.'

Murt cleared his throat. 'Well done, but,' he said to Jamie, and raised his drink.

'The best day of your life,' Breedge said, 'is the day you realise it's no longer your own.'

Eileen drank too much because everyone drank too much. It was Nugent's fault; Nugent was being stealthily and lethally generous, nipping to the bar to conjure rounds between rounds, pre-empting other people as their turn to buy approached. When he wasn't buying drinks, he was sitting at his spot at the far end of the horseshoe-shaped booth, his rigid hands curled either side of his drink, sipping with a straw at his Jameson-and-ice and looking so pleased with himself he seemed almost tearful. Eileen went to the toilet and came back to the bar determined to order a round, her drunkenness like a patiently smouldering fire in the back of her head that she did not, as yet, have to address putting out. Jamie was there, heavy-lidded, breathing through his nose like a stabled horse.

'Your mother is in some way with the news,' Eileen said.

'She is processing,' Jamie said.

'You are going to be fine.'

'Are you fine?'

'What?'

'Never mind me. Are you fine, Eileen?'

'I am.'

'I know you are,' Jamie said, his mouth gone beady, unrepentant with drink. 'You are armour-plated.'

'I'm what?' Eileen said.

'You are a tank, Eileen. You just smash over things and you keep going.'

'What's that mean?'

'Murt. That boy is struggling, in case you didn't know.'

'I do know.'

'If I were in your shoes I know what I'd be saying. I'd be saying that I am trying to help. But you have to take your boot off his throat. Just for a little while you have to take your boot off his throat.'

Eileen's body felt like a heavy coat she had neglected to remove, the blood in her face thick and clambering. She went to speak but her throat shied.

'Murt is my best friend. I care so much about Murt,' she was able to finally say in a thin, winded voice, as if she were trying to talk after a bout of sprinting.

'You care for him, Eileen,' Jamie said, 'but you have no pity for him. He is what he is. He is not like the rest of us. You have to accept that. You have to have a little pity.'

'I don't know what Murt wants. But I don't think he wants pity, not from me,' Eileen said.

Jamie turned himself around, placed an elbow on the bar. He looked toward their booth. The table was honeycombed with empties. Sara, Breedge, Murt, and Nugent all looked wired and exhausted.

'Murt will be moving back in with the mother shortly, did he tell you?'

'No,' Eileen said.

'That's why she's come out, really. Babby aside. It's difficult, but they are friends again.'

'I think that's good, anyway,' Eileen said.

'Do you know why Murt went back into the hospital? Do you know why he came to stay with Nuge and us, which was, by the way, my idea?'

Eileen said nothing.

'Living with Murt? Give me a break. Just try it someday, Eileen. She rang me up the night he went back into the hospital and you know what she said to me? She said, "He had to go." She said, "It was me or it was him." Imagine having to say that about your own son.'

'Think what you like about me,' Eileen said.

'You tell me what's best for that boy,' Jamie said.

Eileen said nothing. Jamie took a drink of his drink.

'There is no best.'

The following week Murt moved back in with his mother and a fortnight after that Jamie and Sara got the go-ahead to move in with Sara's folks. The Duanes despised Jamie but for the sake of the baby they assented to having him under their roof. At Nugent's behest, Jamie left his car in his uncle's care. Nugent pleaded a convincing case: there was plenty of parking space and he would be happy to keep the tank topped up and take it for the occasional spin. Nugent's own car was an unsalvageable relic, the tires flat, gummed to the ground. It was Jamie's car Nugent used. He tried a week after Jamie and Sara left, on a Sunday evening, guiding the car into the cobweb-raftered garage at the back of his house and running a length of amputated garden hose from the exhaust pipe in through the driver's window. He drank heavily beforehand and swallowed a dozen sleeping pills. Once he had the engine on, he tried to cover up the gap in the driver's window with masking tape, but peeling away the required length of tape proved too difficult, what mobility he still possessed baffled by the pills and the booze and the carbon monoxide swilling around his head: eventually he passed out, but he vomited the pills in his sleep and the garage was not an airtight enough structure to accommodate a sufficient buildup of gas. It was Murt who found him. He was dropping in a spare plate of roast dinner from his mother's and just said he knew, coming through the unlocked front door of the house, some charge to the untidy emptiness within: a clear bag of defrosted chicken thighs puddling in the sink, a cup with a cracked handle lying in a cold splat of tea on the floor, the door out to the back ajar.

'The garage door was down. Do you remember if the garage door is ever usually down? I don't know, but maybe that was it. Subliminally, maybe it was like I registered that. I went out and realised I could hear an engine. I got the door up and he was within, in the car. He looked inhuman. Face on him like week-old cat shit.'

Murt telling this to Eileen the Friday after he found Nugent, Nugent stabilised in the I.C.U. in Galway, breathing on his own but still very frail, waking only briefly and not communicating when he did, the doctors as yet dicey on the prospective degree of brain damage, organ damage, everything. Eileen and Murt were in Staunton's, Eileen on Sprite, Murt on Guinness. Eileen had the day off. Murt had enrolled in an evening writing class held in the secondary school, and had a session later.

'Jamie's awful cut up about the car.'

'You would be,' Eileen said.

'I think he feels duped.'

'How's Sara?'

'She's good. They'd the first scan. The what you call. The sonogram. The womb. Might as well be footage of the moon.' Murt supped his Guinness. 'Jamie's insisting now he wants to sell the car. He says getting into it feels like climbing into someone's tomb.'

'Nugent's alive.'

'He gave it some try, though.'

'He won't get much for that yoke at this stage,' Eileen said. 'Scrappage, is my guess. Come up tonight, though. Mark's birthday. We're having people.'

'He says there's a cursed energy to the car now. A malignant charge, when he gets in,' Murt said.

'How's the writing class?'

'The class is fine. Sound skins. Everyone is seventy, but they bring in homemade scones every week.'

'Well, there you go,' Eileen said.

The party had been going for several hours by the time Murt showed. Eileen saw his head bobbing in the crowded sitting room. She picked up a bottle of Guinness and made her way toward him, stepping carefully over Ashleigh, sprawled with four other kids on the ground in front of the TV, refereeing who went next on the Xbox.

Murt saw her, put his head down, shouldered a channel toward her.

'Brought these with me if you don't mind,' Murt said. Two women and a man were following him. They were all old.

'Oh, God, of course not, love!'

'This is Freda, this is Margaret, and this is Tom,' Murt said. 'Everybody, this is Eileen.'

The women were smiling but looked a little apprehensive. Around them people heedlessly jostled and cawed.

'Come on and I'll get you a drink,' Eileen said gently.

'Go on, they're my crowd to babysit, I'll get them a drink,' Murt said.

Eileen let him go. Mark appeared beside her, slid his arm around her waist. 'Who on earth invited the biddies?'

'Murt brought them.'

'Murt. Well, fair play,' Mark said.

Some of Mark's friends produced a guitar and a squeezebox. They played 'Sally MacLennane' and 'The Sick Bed of Cuchulainn', 'Johnny Jump Up' and 'Solsbury Hill' and 'Leave Me Alone'.

Mark found Danny hiding out in his bedroom, and cajoled him downstairs, trumpet in hand. Danny was dressed for bed, striped pajama bottoms and an Argentina jersey with MESSI 10 on the back. He stood in the little clearing in the living room where the other musicians were seated, laconically tuning and adjusting their instruments. Danny kept his head down and transferred his weight from foot to foot, working a kind of stage stoicism. People began to shout 'Come on, lad!' and 'Go on, Danny!,' Mark proudly trying to shush people. Danny tapped his foot tentatively until the crowd noise dropped to a murmur, and with no ceremony whomped out a couple of big baggy notes, just to settle the air around him. 'Hang on, now,' he said. He set his stance again, and began to play. He wagged his shoulders in time with the music, his cheeks inflating and hollowing, the exertions corrugating his brow, but his eyes, even as they jumped around, maintained an ironical gaze, unimpressed and forbearing, as if the noise filling up the room had nothing to do with him. But he was concentrating, you could see it in his fingers – the way they caged and danced against the trumpet's curved and tapered body, which opened out into the startling, brassy, orchidaceous mouth of the bell.

He'd played this one before. Eileen liked it.

Tom – the man who'd come in with Murt – was standing beside Eileen, nursing a bottle of Coors. He had the solid, weather-beaten features and wary demeanour of a farmer on a visit to town.

'Now, that's good,' Tom said.

'He is good,' Eileen said.

'Chet Baker,' Tom said.

'What?'

'The tune. It's by Chet Baker. "Let's Get Lost." That's the good stuff, Eileen.'

'How are you finding Murt?'

'It's good to have new blood in the group. Lord knows we need periodic freshening up.'

'Is he any good?'

'At what?'

'At the writing, I suppose.'

Tom smiled. 'I'd say Colm Tóibín won't be quaking in his boots anytime soon. But sure look, as long as you're getting something out of it. He's a fine young man, all told. Getting something out of it is the main thing. That's why the rest of us are there.'

'How long have you been in the group?'

'Oh, now. Twelve years, I'd say. We've a decent core of regulars. Adherents, like them two lunatics.' Tom nodded at the women, who were standing with Murt. The women were talking and Murt was watching them, smiling, intent. 'Other ones come and go, younger ones. Women mainly, of course. There's only two regular men, myself included, and a good ten ladies. It's harder for the young to stick with things. They've other tacks to be chasing, sooner or later.'

'Twelve years,' Eileen said. 'That's a fair stint.'

'We are the terminal cases now, is what we tell ourselves. We'd a smashing woman, died of cancer coming on a year ago. She was a fine woman and she was a very gifted poet. First of the set to go. That's the joke now. We are in it to the end.'

'Sorry to hear that,' Eileen said.

'Don't be.' Tom said. 'That's life. But it doubles your resolve in some way, do you know?'

Eileen said nothing, because he didn't require an answer. Tom took a drink of his beer.

'That boy can play something beautiful. You must be proud,' Tom said, and Eileen thought that even though Danny was good, he was perhaps not so good that it merited this string of compliments. Eileen figured the man was just being agreeable, decently filling the silence, the way you had to with a stranger.

'What else would I be?' Eileen said.

Slow Gut Instinct:

Colin Barrett on 'Whoever is There, Come on Through'

Colin Barrett's debut collection *Young Skins* won the Guardian First Book Award, the Frank O'Connor International Short Story Award and the Rooney Prize for Irish Literature. His second collection *Homesickness* made *The New York Times* 100 Notable Books of the Year 2022 and was a book of the year in *Oprah Daily* and *The Irish Times*.

In our conversation, Colin spoke about his use of instinct instead of keeping to a structure in his writing.

What was your first impulse to write this story?

I wrote that first scene first, and, by the time I had described Eileen in the car and the man she was looking at, I had an idea of their dynamic.

It was the first scene I thought of and it ended up still being the first scene by the time I'd finished, which I suppose is not that unusual for me. It doesn't always happen that way, sometimes the first thing you think of ends up being moved.

What was it in this scene that felt like it had a story in it? What potential did it contain for you?

I tend to think visually. I try to think most of my stories start with a scene that's pregnant with possibility and is one or two degrees off from what you might expect the scene to be. In this case it was Eileen meeting this fella Murt, picking him up from the bus station, though she's not his partner, she's not a close family member, she's a friend and I just had that sense she was smoking a cigarette and a little bit apprehensive. He was obviously a little bit nervous too; he was wandering around, the last guy left at the station, a little bit helpless-looking – everything just came out of that sort of configuration. No dialogue, no real idea of the exact nature of their relationship but just the almost-distinct body language of these two characters, separate but in a scene together.

Did you work out the story as you went along then?

Yeah, the story started off as a short commission for the radio. It was only going to be a thousand words, just the opening scene of Murt getting into the car and driving to a McDonalds on the way to his uncle's house. Just that initial scene and the dialogue, the back and forth, him commenting on the architecture of the town's buildings; all of that stuff came pretty naturally, it just flowed.

The radio people didn't take it because it was too depressing – it was meant to be a Christmas story and here's this story about a lad who's come out of a mental health facility. I got a very nice message saying: 'thanks, but I don't think we can do this for Christmas.'

I thought there was more in it though so I just kept going at it, the next step always being one degree off from what you'd expect; for example, instead of bringing Murt back to his mother's house, he's going to his uncle's house and I had to think why would she be taking him to his uncle's house, why is he not going to his mother, which was the next puzzle to work out – eventually I realised he had a domineering bigger brother named Jamie and the rest of it just flowed out of there.

You were posing questions and solving them as you went?

Yeah, I don't know how else to do it really. I definitely don't think architecturally. I don't think too far ahead, I don't think as conceptually as I know some people do, I just move by instinct, by slow gut instinct.

Sometimes I go down a wrong path and I have to turn around and come back, so all I feel I'm doing is following vague notions, like dim lights in the distance. It's a very practical thing, there's not a particular technical or philosophical reason or anything else behind it.

I like the idea of having to try and give the reader everything they need in the story in the present moment, as the story is unfolding. I try not to overdo backstory, or exposition, thinking 'what can I leave out' – it's important in short stories because you don't need three pages of backstory on Eileen or Murt growing up. You can sneak that stuff in as you unfold the story in the present moment. That's what keeps me interested – just chasing some notion in the story. It's a feeling or mood I'm after, rather than anything important or interesting to say about the characters or society or anything else.

The first difficulty in a story is getting a sense of what that particular mood is and the second difficulty is getting it down and bringing as much of it onto the page. That's what I do.

So, for example, the scene with Keith Cullen seemed quite a particular decision. Was this arrived at instinctively or was it more a conscious inclusion?

From my perspective, it just arrived. I was not thinking weeks in advance that there's going to be a scene where they encounter some guy they went to school with and all that illuminated more about Murt and their relationship when they were younger. I realised that's what the scene could be when I happened upon it but I didn't really think too much beyond just having the idea for it. Belleek woods is a real place down in Mayo, it's near a river, pretty much as I depicted it, a very moody and evocative place especially if the weather's like that – harsh and wintry. So I just put them there and the scene came along – it seemed more interesting if they knew the jogger than if they didn't. Everything in a short story carries a lot of weight, almost all a kind of symbolic weight, even if you're trying to write a straight realistic story. I like that about it, it means you've got to be very careful about what you put in and what you leave out.

Kevin was useful, he wasn't just a jogger running by for a bit of colour, he became a way to give the reader more about their relationship.

In another interview, you said that: 'Eileen, I think, actually likes her life, or likes enough of the things in it, Murt included. In fiction, maybe that's a sin.' What was it like making a story from such slight dramatic resources?

I find it a challenge but I'm always interested in it. That is not to say, I'm always thinking, 'How little story can I provide here.' I want to give them a story and I want to give them events and I want things to happen. I don't want them to starve for engagement.

The people I write about again and again are people from small towns. Everyone has to live inside a very finite circumscribed reality most of the time and I guess I'm just as fascinated by pattern as by the breaking of it. In most of my stories, part of the fun seems to be setting up the routines, the mundanity of someone's life, their relationships and whatever else. Most stories are about deviation from a pattern, or breaking it – my tendency is instead to think, 'How much of this can I keep?'

This story was never about Eileen or Murt's life blowing up. I was trying to just show these two people trying to look out for each other in a basically loving positive relationship, if not completely healthy, as damn near practically, enough to get both people through.

I wanted to show it was fraught. There's latent dynamics as well as what's happening on the surface, like any relationship or friendship. That is the stuff that interests me. I'm always trying to get into that area. I still feel when I read novels or short stories, even in the ones I love, I feel there's still so much actual life missing from this stuff. The best writing captures something of all of that but there's so much of it that's not in books or stories.

Life is so fucking uncanny. I'm not even talking about the weird stuff, but everyday reality: the kind of thoughts you have, the weird shapes and textures that can come into a friendship or a relationship, again not caused by anything overdramatic but just the strange shape of it all.

You said you try not to overdo the backstory, and you've said before that there is a thrilling possibility, a freedom, in the idea of not telling the characters' backstory. What does this free you to *do*?

I generally know the backstory of my characters as I'm writing. Then I see how much I can leave out.

Generally, editors say: 'please put in more, explain what the exact nature of this thing is – is it going to kill anybody just to put in a line or two just to help the reader.' I think that's totally fair.

I want to see how much I can get in by implication, so that when I show that story to someone else I trust, like an editor, and they say this is great but we need just a little bit more in here, then I go and put it in, which is probably the reverse of how you are meant to do it.

I had another short story called 'The Ways' – about Pell, an orphan who lives with her older brother who's her legal guardian. In the first draft of that I literally didn't put any of that in because it didn't come up organically in the story; it wasn't in the immediate action, so I just left it out. The editors said I should probably put in the reason why the parents are not there, which was fair. But I wanted to write about someone in grief and part of grief is repression and not thinking about it so I left that out. *I* knew she was an orphan because the parents hadn't run off somewhere, they were dead, but I left it out of the story to try and see how far I could get before I had to put it in.

My reluctance with backstory is not that I think people don't have them or that a coherent character is an illusion, it's just a question of how much I can put into the story without making it explicit.

So you feel backstory gets in the way of the current 'moment' of the narrative?

I know a reader needs flow and information, but as a writer I think you can get bogged down in thinking about the exact nature of something absent.

I think with someone like Eileen, who has had a tumultuous romantic entanglement, I wanted it just to stay in the background rather than being a point of contention. It's a story about family and different configurations of familiar relationships and I think I've given the reader enough in the story as it is presented.

You need to know about Murt and Eileen's relationship but you don't really need to know about her relationship with her husband. It's not as big a deal as what is in there.

The characters in this are intensely particular people. What work did you go through with them to get them to how they appear in the final draft?

I was lucky with these characters. They sort of all flowed out, they were just there. I can never get mystical about this stuff but sometimes characters do arrive, you know. Like you realise you need someone and they come.

The story is fairly cluttered with characters, as stories go, but the way in was through the dialogue, bringing them in and having them speaking and interacting, like that stuff with the doughnuts. That's what you're always trying to chase, they're talking about this thing but hopefully you're learning so much about them even though they're just talking about this trivial thing.

Even though the characters came fully formed, you still have to find a way to move the story on. Writing it, I found I had Murt and Eileen but I didn't want to go straight to his mother, I didn't want it to become some Oedipal thing, so I said, 'He's going to stay with his uncle', and then I thought I'd need a contrast to shed light on the nature of Eileen and Murt's relationship – which was Jamie and his girlfriend, Sarah.

What proved the greatest challenge in the writing of this?

I do have a great faith when I'm writing a story, I always think it is going to go somewhere and be good, but I suppose the most difficult thing here was establishing a pattern and routine.

After the opening sequence when we meet everyone, there's then a transitional phase where they go into routine and I'm basically summarising what's been happening; Eileen has organised her shifts so she can be with Murt – it's the most mundane part of writing in a sense, when I'm just moving things along. I find it difficult to gauge, to get the balance right and know when I should summarise and move on, and when I should dramatise, actually depict a scene. The reader has to buy that these two have been friends for years and there's a dynamic there, a well worn one, without it being either boring and or blown up.

When you re-read this story now, what do you think of it?

It doesn't feel that long ago for me. It's a story I'm really proud of. It was a story that moved me onto a different phase of my writing. I expect if we were talking about one of the stories in *Young Skins* I would be a lot more critical. A lot of them were written in 2010 and 2011 so I'd be a lot more critical of my much younger self than my slightly younger self.

I had a sense this was really promising when I started it, but I wanted to get it right. I don't think it's perfect or anything, but in capturing these slightly skewed, slightly off relationships – not only between Murt and Eileen but in the dynamic between Murt and his brother – I was able to more or less execute what I wanted to with the story.

For me the prose has evolved from my writing in *Young Skins*. It's the kind of writing I've been leaning more to with the novel [*Wild Houses*, published by Faber] and certainly in subsequent stories I've written.

I'm proud of it. If someone asked me what's one story I should read by me, I'd tell them to read this one.

With the birthday party scene at the end I wondered if bringing people together like this was something of a climax, something like a ritual or spectacle? Why did you choose this scene and close with that final exchange with Eileen?

It was just the way the story was coming along and the fact that I had a big cast – they don't all end up at the party but it felt like they could have.

Although the story has some bleak elements in it, I was trying to write about a basically positive loving relationship, one that's platonic and defies easy definition. Eileen is someone who's okay with life which is maybe unusual, she's not fighting against anything overtly, though she is in her own way, which Jamie spots.

With the party at the end, I decided, 'Let's just do that', and it flowed from the actual composition, my writing of the story; once her partner's son, Danny – who can play the trumpet – was introduced, I thought we'd have him do a bit of music at the end. I just wanted to end positively.

The little exchange that Eileen has at the end with this other guy, was just a simple trick – bringing in another character allows a slightly different perspective on the things you've already seen and characters you've already witnessed. As well as just a reaffirmation of Eileen's essential soundness and consideration and quiet pride in her own life and the people in her life.

Like an answer to Jamie's earlier accusation?

Though Jamie's accusation can't be discounted. It's not right or wrong necessarily – he's not the most reliable gauge – but I thought it was an interesting thing to put in there. She *may* be perpetrating what Jamie accuses her of, but nobody's just one thing and this brings it home that she's fundamentally a decent person.

What did you learn in the writing of this story?

In my own boring artistic evolution it did feel separate from the one that came before, as well as to what was coming after. I haven't really changed my subject matter all that much but my approach to the material – the mood and intensity I'm looking for – I was able to find in that story. That's what I learnt, that the *ways* you want to tell stories can change and evolve.

Had your previous stories been written in a different way?

All my stories have been a bit chaotic. The stories in *Young Skins* for instance all happened in the same place so they were all unified by that and to me they are tightly focused on a certain type of person or versions of types of people.

Someone may say it's the same fucking stuff as in *Young Skins* but to me the characters were more considered. *Young Skins* is a younger person's book; it's full of brash, wild things happening and that's great, that's the book it is. I'm happy it's that way but this is a bit quieter and more diffuse, looking at transitional stages.

Was your evolution influenced by any writers you were reading at the time?

I was reading a lot more of Alice Munro and John MacGahern who I hadn't read a lot of. Joy Williams was a huge influence on me, and Sally Rooney's short stories interested me a lot; she was doing interesting things in those. There's an American writer called Tom Drury [who appears in *Reverse Engineering II*], whose novel, *The End of Vandalism,* is basically a collection of short stories.

In Alice Munro's earlier collections her writing is Updike-ian, hyper-detailed and specific and alive to every texture. But descriptively in terms of metaphor and simile, I would say it's better, it has much more control than John Updike, more interest in people. Then you watch her as she develops and her style begins to pare back and pare back. She could do all the technical, baroque stuff but she stopped because for her it was about getting closer to the characters, and closer to the story.

It was incredible, when I started reading her chronologically, seeing that was an important moment. Hopefully that will impact me for years. It may not be detectable in that story but that was an important thing to happen for me.

Acknowledgements

Victory Lap by George Saunders
Taken from *Tenth of December* by George Saunders, published by Bloomsbury Publishing Plc. Copyright © George Saunders, 2013.

The Gloves Are Off by Claire-Louise Bennett
Copyright © 2015, Claire-Louise Bennett, used by permission of Fitzcarraldo Limited.

The Bunker by Mark Haddon
Taken from *Dogs and Monsters* by Mark Haddon published by Chatto & Windus. Copyright © Mark Haddon, 2024. Reprinted by permission of The Random House Group Limited.

Agata's Machine by Camilla Grudova
Copyright © 2017, Camilla Grudova, used by permission of Fitzcarraldo Limited.

Mr Blythe Esq. by Amber Medland
Copyright © 2021, Amber Medland. First published in *The Drift* magazine.

Whoever is There, Come on Through by Colin Barrett
Taken from *Home Sickness* by Colin Barrett, published by Jonathan Cape. Copyright © Colin Barrett, 2022. Reprinted by permission of The Random House Group Limited.